PoisonBuried Punch

A Black Cat Cafe Cozy Mystery Series

by Lyndsey Cole

Chapter 1

It all started because Leona was so competitive.

Annie's heart almost stopped when she opened her door and found Christy standing in front of her, covered in blood.

"What happened?" Annie lurched toward her friend.

"Call Tyler," Christy said before she slumped on the top step.

Annie searched for her phone. Of course it wasn't where she usually left it and her mind was a frozen blank. It rang. She dashed to her counter, pushing papers out of the way to uncover it before it stopped ringing. She grabbed her phone, grateful to recognize Tyler's number pop up on her screen.

Without even saying hello, she blurted out, "Tyler, get here quickly. Something happened to Christy."

Rushing back to the door, Annie's mouth fell open. All that met her gaze was empty space where Christy had fallen.

Annie paced liked a caged lion, waiting for the approaching siren. What should she do? Search for Christy or wait for Tyler?

Before she could make a decision, Tyler's cruiser was in her driveway. Annie couldn't believe her eyes.

Tyler walked toward Annie's apartment with a laughing Christy tucked under his arm.

"I wish you could have seen your face," Christy said as she bounded up the steps and walked into Annie's apartment followed by Tyler. He shrugged as he walked by as if to say he didn't have anything to do with the prank.

Annie's brain couldn't catch up with her eyes and ears. "You're okay?" She stared at Christy's blood splattered clothes. Christy Crank, the detective in Catfish Cove, and Tyler Johnson, the Chief of Police, weren't known for having a sense of humor.

Christy calmly gazed around Annie's tidy apartment as she threw a handful of roasted pumpkin seeds into her mouth. She offered the bag to Annie. "We wanted to test our Halloween costumes on an unsuspecting victim." Christy pulled Tyler close, aiming a long plastic dagger at his chest. "Can you guess what we are?

"Umm, you're the bad guy? But I can't figure out what Tyler is supposed to be." Annie held her hand over her mouth to hide a grin.

Tyler frowned and looked down at his police uniform. "Really? I'm supposed to be a cop."

Christy and Annie burst out laughing and Tyler's face blushed a deep shade of pink. Annie munched on some pumpkin seeds and handed the bag back to Christy.

"Oh, you were teasing me, weren't you Annie?" He put his arm around Christy's waist. "We're going to the Halloween party together."

Annie cocked her right eyebrow. "Oh, really? Something tells me this may be more than a date?"

Tyler blushed again but remained silent. Christy smiled and wiggled her eyebrows.

"I see," Annie said, even though she wasn't at all sure about what was going on between Detective Christy Crank and Police Chief Tyler Johnson. Annie felt a tiny bit protective of Tyler since they had once been engaged and were now good friends. Annie hoped Christy didn't lead Tyler on and break his fragile heart, especially after his recent breakup with Annie's childhood friend, JC.

"Is the pre-party still on at Jason's house at five?" Christy asked.

"Yup." Annie nodded. "He's supposed to be finding me a costume. Dressing up is *not* exactly my cup of tea but I told him I'd be a good sport."

"My goal is to win the prize for best couples costume at the Catfish Cove Pub," Christy said as she looked Tyler up and down. "I'm not sure anyone will be impressed with *his* outfit, though."

"What? It's perfect." Tyler looked at Christy in complete shock.

"Yeah, yeah, yeah. At any rate, my costume worked on Annie." Christy looped her arm in Tyler's crooked elbow. "We'll see you later at Jason's house. Can't wait to see what he comes up with for you both. And I know Leona has her heart set on winning. Has she always been so competitive?"

Both Annie and Tyler laughed.
"Competitive? No, not in the least," Annie said, her voice full of sarcasm. Her birth mother was known for always wanting to be in the limelight and she went all out to win any competition she jumped into.

Annie returned to her baking after they left and a quiet peace returned to her apartment. She promised Jason she'd bring a dessert to the party and decided to make her favorite recipe, which, hands-down, was her pumpkin pie. At least for this time of year—Halloween. Anything pumpkin was yummy, but her pie was easy and delicious. Her mouth started to water thinking about the blend of cinnamon and nutmeg mixed into the freshly baked pumpkin she still had from the last farmer's market of the season.

With the pie in the oven and the timer set, Annie had enough time to shower and change. Dressed in her comfiest jeans and long sleeve t-shirt, Annie was ready to take

Roxy for a walk on the Lake Trail along Heron Lake.

She peaked in the oven to see how the pie was coming along just as the timer buzzed.

"Perfect," she said as she breathed in the rush of delicious aroma. The top was solid with a small crack.

Roxy sat anxiously by the front door, looking at Annie with her head cocked to one side and her irresistible puppy dog eyes following Annie's every move.

With the pie cooling on the counter, Annie hooked Roxy to her leash and headed out the door. She zipped her fleece-lined sweatshirt as high as it would go and pulled the hood over her head. The temperature had dropped significantly and the wind was blowing steadily since she was last outside. Late October weather in Catfish Cove was just as likely to be windy and cold as pleasantly cool.

She walked quickly, hoping to generate some extra heat while Roxy trotted along, sniffing what only her dog nose could smell. Annie wrapped her arms tightly around herself to keep from shivering. After about fifteen minutes, she called Roxy and turned around, heading back toward Jason's Cobblestone Cottage and her apartment. She hoped he had a nice, toasty fire in his fireplace to warm her chilled body.

As she turned up the path to his porch, she smiled at his carved jack-o-lanterns with candlelight flickering through the designs. She made a quick detour across the driveway, up the stairs to her apartment over Jason's garage, and grabbed her pie before walking in his side door.

A gust of cold air followed her into Jason's house, but as soon as she closed the door, she smelled the wood fire and felt the warmth from the cozy blaze. Jason already had several small pumpkins on his long table, filled with beautiful fall flowers. Black candles were spaced between the pumpkins, and gauzy webbing hung from the beams like a giant spider web.

He held a mug of warm cider toward Annie. "This will take the chill off. I added some rum but you can put in more if you want to."

Annie sipped the drink, watching Jason walk to his closet door. She enjoyed the view of his well-proportioned backside and smiled to herself. "This will do for now. I don't want to get too wobbly before the night has even begun."

"I have a surprise for you," Jason said as he took a hanger off the back of the door. "I found the perfect costumes for us."

With great ceremony, he unveiled a long gown, crown, high-heeled shoes, and elbow length white gloves.

Annie chugged the rest of her cider. "A princess? I've never seen myself in *that* role."

"No, a queen." He pulled the cover off the other hanger. "And a king for me. We're hosting this small party so we should be king and queen. Don't you think that's appropriate?"

Annie laughed. "It's a hideous purple. It will clash with my strawberry blond hair."

Jason gently placed the crown over Annie's curls. She shook her head. A few unruly spirals found their way over the crown and tickled her face. Jason tucked the curls back in place.

"It's a costume. Besides, purple was the only color left. You'll be beautiful. As always." He straightened the crown and stole a kiss. "And the crown definitely goes with your diamond earrings."

Annie leaned into his warm embrace. "Let's lock the doors, turn off the lights and maybe everyone will just go straight to the party at the Catfish Cove Pub."

"Okay." Jason headed toward the door to lock it but Annie laughed.

"I was only kidding."

He stuck his lower lip out in a pout. "Maybe after the party?"

She smiled and nodded before they gathered up the costumes and got changed. Jason added his crown moments before the door opened.

Leona and Danny swooped inside. They made an adorable couple, and Annie wondered if they had set a date yet for their wedding. No sense asking, since Leona would shout it from the highest rooftop once any plans were made.

Danny made an interesting contrast, with green webbed hands looking like a dapper frog, to Leona's princess costume in the same gown as Annie was wearing, except the emerald green version.

Annie and Leona stared at each other. "You got the color I should have," Annie said in a mock angry voice. "But, I have the awesome crown," she said, tilting it a little to one side.

Leona curtsied. "Thanks." She linked her arm through Danny's frog arm, pulling him to Jason's table. Her gown swooshed as she moved carefully, arranging a basket full of cheeses and crackers around a luscious pastry filled with brie and raspberries. "Is this your pumpkin pie Annie?" she asked, pointing to the pie in the center of the table.

Annie nodded. "Yup. I'll cut it in tiny slivers so everyone can try it."

Another blast of cold air swept through the room as Martha and Harry arrived. Harry wore a patch over one eye and carried Charlie, the parrot, in his cage. Martha carried a tray covered with drinks in one hand while she curtsied and fanned her apron with the other.

"Ooh. A pirate and barmaid. There's going to be some stiff competition for best couple," Annie said.

"Martha and Harry are cheating with the extra accessories," Leona complained.

"More like having the best imagination." Martha tipped the tray showing how she glued the glasses to it.

As if on cue, Charlie squawked, "Wanna drink?"

Harry pushed his eye-patch up so he could see better. "I taught him to say that."

Tyler arrived dressed in his police uniform. "Christy isn't here yet?"

"No," Leona answered. "Where's your costume?"

"What you see is what you get." Tyler spread his arms out. "It works way better with Christy in her costume next to me, right Annie?"

"Definitely. Where is she?" Annie cut her pie into eight triangles.

He shrugged. "She said she would meet me here. Something about meeting her ex and her dog, Blue."

Shivers traveled up Annie's arm. "She went alone?"

Tyler nodded. "Why?"

"Just a feeling about—"

The door opened. Christy stood motionless with a white face. Her hands hung down.

Tyler smiled as he approached her. "I think you missed your calling. You're enjoying this killer role way too much."

Christy didn't move. "I stabbed Eddie."

Tyler put his arm around her. "You're letting all the cold air in." He walked her inside and closed the door. "I think everyone understands your costume, you don't have to act it out anymore. It's kind of creepy."

"She's not acting," Annie said, concern lacing her voice. "Eddie's your ex?"

Christy nodded, looking down at the knife in her hand. With blood on it.

Tyler's face blanched. "That's not the fake knife." He took it from Christy.

Annie guided her to the couch. "What happened?" Annie asked, keeping her voice soft and soothing.

Jason handed Christy a glass of water. "Sip this. Don't try to talk yet."

Christy held the glass but it didn't make it to her lips. She stared at Annie. "He tricked me into meeting him. He said he would give Blue back to me."

Tyler sat close to Christy on her other side, silent.

Annie crouched down at eye level with Christy. She held the water glass to Christy's lips. "Take a sip."

Christy did as instructed. Everyone else waited like statues, afraid to move and upset Christy.

Annie took the glass, setting it on the coffee table. "You met Eddie?" she prompted.

"It sounded safe enough. He said to meet him at the Cove's Corner parking lot and he'd bring Blue. I've been waiting for this for the last six months. That must have clouded my judgment." Her hands fidgeted in her lap, twisting one way, then the other. "He didn't bring Blue."

"Where did you get the knife?" Annie asked.

"Eddie had it. He lunged toward me and somehow I ended up with the knife and my defensive training must have kicked in. He fell." Christy looked around Jason's house. "I don't even remember driving here."

"Did you kill him?" Annie held her breath, dreading the answer.

"I stabbed him and he fell. I panicked and didn't even check for a pulse." She finally looked at Tyler. "You need to investigate. I'll wait here."

Tyler nodded. As the Police Chief of Catfish Cove, he had to find out what happened. Even if it meant his detective, Christy Crank, was the murderer.

After Tyler left, Leona poured wine for everyone. Jason put on music and they all tried to pretend they were having a good time.

Charlie squawked, "Wanna drink?" It broke the tension a bit for everyone but Christy.

Leona pulled Annie into the kitchen. "What are we going to do? This will ruin the party tonight."

Annie replied, "You should still go. I'll stay here with Christy until Tyler gets back."

"Nice try Annie. I know what you're doing. You never liked wearing costumes. Although, I will stand out better if you're not there with the same dress." Leona smiled, trying to cheer Annie up. "Even if it *is* that ugly purple."

Jason came in looking for another bottle of wine. "What are you two cooking up in here?"

Leona huffed. "Annie's trying to get out of going to the Halloween party."

Jason uncorked the bottle. "I'll stay here with Annie and Christy. The rest of you should go to the party and we'll come as soon as we can."

"Well, all right. I hate to miss a good time," Leona said as she smoothed her gown.

Jason handed the wine to Leona. "Tell everyone to start eating the food you brought. The Halloween party at the Catfish Cove Pub starts in a half hour."

Before Leona had a chance to pour any wine, Tyler burst through the door. "There's no body at the Cove's Corner parking lot. Christy, are you sure you stabbed him?"

Her mouth fell open. "No body? Did you find any blood?"

Tyler shook his head. "Nothing."

Christy stood up. "If he's not dead, he couldn't have gotten far on his own two feet. Someone must have moved him."

Chapter 2

Annie called Roxy to her side. "We're coming with you," she said to Tyler and Christy.

"Right," Jason added, not sure if Annie's 'we' meant him or her faithful dog but suspected she was referring to Roxy.

"What about the Halloween party?" Leona whined in a voice that sounded like a three year old. "This is my favorite time of year and I plan to win the couples competition."

"Go! Have fun!" Annie replied, turning her back to Leona and struggling to pull her fleece-lined sweatshirt over her purple gown before giving up. "I'm not going out looking for a body in this thing. Don't leave without me," she ordered.

Jason had already shed his costume and it only took Annie a minute to reappear in her comfy clothes. "Let's go."

Jason, Annie, and Roxy followed Tyler's police cruiser to the mostly deserted Cove's Corner parking lot.

Annie couldn't help but feel the dread settle in the pit of her stomach. She and Christy hadn't always been friends, and only a few months earlier she wouldn't have thought twice about Christy's problems. But that was then and this was now.

Christy was the first out of Jason's car, turning her head back and forth. She pointed to a dark corner. "That's where Eddie fell."

Roxy pulled against the leash, dragging Annie to the spot Christy pointed out—a shaded corner under tree branches away from the lights. A bag of trash rustled in the breeze and an empty beer can rolled along the pavement.

But there was no body.

The empty bag blew against Annie's leg. Her heart skipped a beat when she saw it was Christy's favorite brand of roasted pumpkin seeds. She stuffed it into her pocket and dashed after Roxy who made a beeline through the trees to the water's edge. Roxy finally eased up the pressure on her leash.

Christy and Tyler followed. Their flashlights blazed and Jason jogged to catch up.

"Did Roxy find something?" Tyler asked.

Christy moved the beam of light slowly along the rocks at the edge of the lake, then back again, going a little farther out over the water. The flashlight stopped. She moved it back a few feet, illuminating a mound of something. "Is that a body?"

Tyler added his light to Christy's, and they could see the outline of a round boulder with water lapping at the edge.

"I'm going to search in a wider circle," Tyler said before walking into the darkness.

Jason took Christy's flashlight and left in the opposite direction.

Christy covered her face. "You must think I'm crazy, saying I stabbed someone and now we can't find a body. It feels like I've entered the twilight zone. Everything around me is normal but I'm going crazy. That's always what happened when I had anything to do with Eddie."

Annie took Christy by the arm and led her to the deck outside the Black Cat Café. Solar lights along the railing gave a muted glow. She pulled out a chair for Christy and sat across the table from her. "What happened between you and Eddie?"

"What *didn't* happen is more like it," Christy said, with her elbows on the table and her chin resting on her hands. She sighed. "I pride myself on being an in-charge kinda person, but Eddie always threw me off my game."

Annie pulled her sweatshirt tighter and waited. Roxy's nose was in the air, sniffing the breeze. The night was filled with the distant voices of conversations, laughter, and music.

"We met in high school. He was the popular guy, the guy every girl had a crush on. He chose me, and he was so nice, considerate, caring. I fell head over heels in love with him, expecting the happily-ever-after story." She paused, gazing into the darkness over Heron Lake. "It's not something that's easy for me to talk about."

"So, it was perfect until it wasn't. Did something happen?" Annie asked.

"Not *something*, more like everything. We got married after I graduated from the police academy. Our honeymoon was fantastic and Eddie surprised me with a puppy when we got home. Blue melted my heart the minute I held him. That's when Eddie's heart flopped to the dark side and his jealousy took over. He couldn't stand for me to be out of his sight." She stared at Annie. "How could I do my job with him always stalking me and accusing me of meeting other men? I was lucky I left when I did even though it meant leaving Blue behind."

Footsteps sounded across the gravel. Christy clutched Annie's arm. Jason's flashlight lit his face and the two women giggled, relieving some of the tension. He sat down between Annie and Christy.

"I walked along the shore for about a quarter mile. Nothing unusual. Did Tyler find anything?"

"He's not back yet," Annie answered.

"I thought he was dead. Someone must have moved him," Christy said, repeating her earlier comment. "There has to be a blood trail. Tomorrow, when it's light, we should be able to find it."

A dog barked.

Christy jumped up. "Blue?"

A big black lab bounded onto the deck. With his paws reaching to her shoulders, Christy stumbled backward, nearly falling over.

"How did you get here, you big galoot?" Christy wrapped her arms around the slobbery dog, tears streaming down her cheeks.

A woman stepped out of the shadows. "I brought him."

"And you are?" Christy demanded in a cold, hard voice.

"Where's Eddie?" The woman asked, ignoring Christy's question but taking in her blood splattered clothes.

Annie stood up next to Christy. "What are you doing here, Samantha?" Her voice was firm but friendly.

"My friend, Eddie, asked me to meet him here with his dog. I'm supposed to be working at the Halloween party but I told him I'd take my break and bring his dog over. Something about giving the dog back to his ex-wife." She looked at Christy and Blue. "You must be the ex? The new detective in town?"

"And I'm still trying to figure out who you are and why you had Blue." Christy stared at Samantha with her legs spread apart, one hand on her hip and the other possessively on Blue's head.

Annie explained to Christy as Tyler hustled onto the deck, "Samantha works at the Catfish Cove Pub. That helps answer who she is, but not why she had your dog."

Samantha put her hands out, palms up. "What's going on here?

Tyler surveyed the scene. "Samantha? Maybe you'd better sit down so we can try to get to the bottom of this. Do you know Eddie Crank?"

Samantha continued to stand, scowling. "Eddie and Blue stayed with me for a few days. What's going on? You all are creeping me out."

"How do you know him?" Jason asked—not unkindly, but expecting a response.

"It's not really any of your business." She glared at Tyler before adding, "We met at the Mixed Drinks Bartender School."

Christy squinted her eyes. "You're the one he used to talk about? His stalker?"

Samantha waved her hand. "All a big misunderstanding."

"We'll continue this discussion later. Follow me," Tyler said. He turned around and walked off the porch, heading toward the water, lighting the way with his flashlight.

Annie waited for Jason to catch up with her and they stayed in the back behind Samantha.

Samantha hesitated, glancing at Annie and Jason. "What are all of you doing here?"

"Looking for Eddie. You'd better follow Jason."

Annie held Jason back and whispered to him, "Stalker? What was Eddie doing staying with her? And how did he find out Christy was working here in Catfish Cove?"

They continued in silence except for the sound of feet shuffling along the sand and the occasional distant laughter that carried over Heron Lake. Lights dotted the shoreline, like eyes watching the small group of people trudging on the wet sand.

Roxy lurched, pulling as far as the leash would allow. Blue, not on a leash, dashed past her. Tyler stood still ahead of everyone else, his light beam aimed at something partially submerged.

"That is not a rock," Christy said. She waded into the water and turned a body over, face up.

"Samantha, take a look. Is this your friend Eddie?" Tyler asked.

Samantha inched forward, looking between Christy and Tyler. Christy aimed her flashlight on Samantha's face, which reflected beads of sweat. Annie shivered and moved closer to Jason.

Christy grabbed Samantha's arm, yanking her closer to the body. "The police chief asked you a question. Is this your friend Eddie?"

Samantha's eyes were big and round as her head nodded up and down.

Tyler was already on his phone calling an ambulance and more backup officers to the scene.

Christy raised her five foot three inches higher on her tiptoes, almost staring into Samantha's eyes. "How did he get over here?"

Samantha's head shook back and forth and she shrugged. "I have no idea," she finally managed to whisper.

Chapter 3

Samantha's body sagged and Tyler caught her as she swayed, breaking her fall to the ground. He leaned her against the cement wall a few feet back from the water.

Christy pulled her hair into a ponytail, all signs of any weakness long gone with her detective persona firmly back in place. She herded Annie and Jason away from the body. "What do you know about Samantha?" she asked.

Annie shrugged. "Not too much. She's lived here for at least a year with a guy named Kyle Bishop. They both work at the Catfish Cove Pub. Kyle switches between cooking and bartending, and Samantha's a bartender. Not friends of mine, but I've seen them around town."

Christy jotted in her notebook. "She's a bartender, huh? That's interesting. Eddie must have stayed in touch with Samantha after the class ended."

"Do you think he knew you were living here?" Jason asked.

Christy tapped her lips with the top of her pen. "Uh huh, I definitely think that." She glanced back toward Samantha.

Tyler approached with a worried expression pasted to his face. He looked at Christy, then Annie and Jason. "Listen, Christy, I know you want to be part of this investigation but it's off limits for you. You admitted to stabbing Eddie. Is there anything else you should tell me?"

Christy's eyes narrowed into slits. Her mouth opened then closed. Her hands curled into tight fists.

Tyler turned back toward Annie. "You two may as well leave. It's going to be crazy around here for a while."

"What about Blue?" Annie gently touched Christy's shoulder to get her attention. Blue sat quietly next to Roxy. "I can take him back to my apartment with Roxy if you aren't going home."

"Yeah. Good idea. I'll know he'll be safe there. Thanks." Christy walked away.

Annie sensed Christy's anger.

Jason held Annie's hand as they made their way through the darkness toward the solar glow on the deck of the Black Cat Café.

Annie asked what was on her mind and she assumed on Jason's too. "Do you think she killed Eddie?"

"Time will answer that fifty million dollar question," Jason said. They continued in silence before Jason changed the subject. "We can drop the dogs off and see what's happening at the Halloween party."

"Do I have to put that hideous costume back on?" Annie knew Jason was trying to distract her from Christy's woes.

"No. It's probably winding down by now anyway. Maybe we can talk to Kyle and get some more information about Eddie." Jason glanced over his shoulder. "There's more to why Eddie was here in town than Christy let on about. I think she's hiding something."

They walked past the deck of the Black Cat café before Annie responded. "Hiding what?"

Jason moved his arm around Annie's shoulder. "If I knew that, we wouldn't have to go on a fishing expedition, would we? What did Christy tell you about Eddie?"

They were almost to the car when Annie stopped. "She said he went from being nice, caring, and considerate in high school to a jealous stalker after the honeymoon. How can someone flip like that?"

He got Annie moving again and opened the car door for her. "That's what we're going to find out. I think Christy might still be in trouble, but I'm not sure if she's aware of the danger. Yet."

Jason opened the back door for the dogs. Blue followed Roxy onto the back seat and sat leaning against the white terrier.

"I hope Blue is okay with cats. Smokey will be curled up on the couch and won't be happy about a big slobbery intruder."

Jason pulled out of the parking lot and headed up the hill to Cobblestone Cottage. "By the looks of him, I don't think much of anything bothers that dog."

Annie took the steps two at a time to her apartment over the garage and opened the door for the dogs. Smokey hissed and stood up with his back arched. Blue looked at him, then at Annie, as if to say 'what's wrong with that little guy?' She patted his head. "Don't worry about the cat. He's all talk."

Annie dumped food into two bowls for the dogs and carried Smokey into her bedroom, just in case. No need to tempt a conflict.

When Annie climbed back into Jason's car, he handed her the crown. "We can compromise with the costume and wear our king and queen crowns. It's better than nothing. And here's something to snack on."

After she parked the crown on her curls, Annie lifted the foil to see a generous slice of her pumpkin pie smothered with whipped cream. "Ooh, good choice."

She dipped a piece of the crust in the cream and stuck it in her mouth. "Do you want a bite?"

"You bet. Your pumpkin pie is my favorite." He opened his mouth so Annie could feed him. They hit a bump and most of the pie ended up smushed around his mouth instead of in it. Using his tongue, Jason cleaned off the mess. "Delicious, even if you're making me work for my treat."

Annie took a big bite for herself with plenty of cream. "Did someone clean up the rest of the food?"

"Yup. The food was put away and the dishes washed. I can't complain."

The street in front of the Catfish Cove Pub was jam packed with cars. "We'll have to walk a bit. Do you mind?" Jason asked Annie.

"Not at all. The longer it takes to get inside, the happier I am."

Jason put his hand on Annie's thigh. "Don't like crowds much?"

"Nope. And a loud costume-wearing crowd is the absolute worst, but I'll survive." She knew her smile was unconvincing.

The noise from the party leaked from the pub and filled the air on Main Street. People in costumes spilled out the door, laughing and getting some fresh air.

The ambulance drove past, in no rush to get to the hospital. Annie and Jason watched, knowing part of the story inside the vehicle, but everyone else carried on as if this night was just like any other.

Jason held the door open and put his hand on Annie's back to support her and give a little nudge of encouragement if necessary.

The pub was packed wall-to-wall. Annie felt her heart rate increase. She scanned the room, wondering if the contest winners had already been announced. Jason helped himself to two drinks off the tray of a passing waiter before they wove farther inside.

Annie elbowed Jason to get his attention, making the beer slosh over the rim of the mugs. "There's Leona." She pointed to a woman in an emerald green gown standing with a group of their friends in the back. "Come on."

Holding the mugs high enough to avoid any disasters, Jason followed Annie. Leona was trying to dance in the tiny space she had available.

"Who won the costume contest?" Annie asked as she leaned in as close as possible to Leona's ear.

"It hasn't been announced yet." Leona hugged Danny. "Martha and Harry will be our closest competition for sure." A furrow formed between Leona's eyebrows. "Where's your costume?"

Annie touched her crown. "Ah, well, it's a long story."

Leona's hand went to her mouth and her eyes grew big and round. "Did you find the guy Christy stabbed?"

"Eventually. It's complicated." Annie sipped her beer. "How well do you know Samantha and Kyle?"

Leona wobbled her hand back and forth. "I see them when I'm in here. Why?"

The deafening noise made it almost impossible to have a conversation. "Samantha is the connection to Christy's ex."

"The dead guy?"

Annie nodded.

"Don't look now, but here comes Kyle. Why don't you ask him a few questions?" Leona suggested.

Kyle stopped next to Leona. "Have any of you seen Samantha? She's supposed to be helping here and she disappeared into thin air."

Annie touched Kyle's arm to get his attention. "What do you know about Eddie Crank?"

Kyle's jaw clenched and his eyes narrowed. "That slimy creep? Why do you ask?"

Annie took a long sip. "When's the last time you saw him?"

Kyle looked around the bar and shrugged. "Earlier? He's been in town for a few weeks and he usually hangs out at the bar annoying everyone. Dennis threatened to ban him if he didn't control his mouth. And his hands. I told Samantha she had to tell him to stop coming to our apartment." He waved to someone across the room. "I've gotta run. If you see Sam, tell her I'm looking for her."

Jason managed to scrounge up a plate of chicken wings and a container of blue cheese for dipping. "This is all I could find. How much food have all these people gone through?"

"Tons," Leona answered. "It's been a great party. So, where's Samantha?"

The DJ turned the music down and played a drum roll. "The time you've all been waiting for is here. The decision for best costume of the night has been made by popular vote."

The crowd hooted and hollered. "Who won? Who won?" rang out from across the pub.

The DJ made a great fanfare opening the envelope. Another drum roll sounded, then he looked out over the crowd and smiled. "The barmaid, pirate, and parrot! Please make your way to me."

More clapping and whistling. Annie glanced at Leona and saw her downcast face. She squeezed Leona's hand, knowing how much Leona loved this type of attention and how disappointed she would be not to win.

The DJ held up his hands. "There's a tie tonight . . ." he paused to let the tension build, "with the princess and the frog!"

Leona's face lit up as she grabbed Danny's webbed hand and pulled him to the stage to stand next to Martha and Harry.

Charlie, Harry's parrot, couldn't stop asking, "Wanna drink?" and the crowd roared for more.

"Here's Dennis to present the prizes," the DJ announced as the owner of the pub made his appearance carrying two carved pumpkins. Candlelight glowed through the intricately carved designs.

Amber, dressed in a man's black business suit, snapped photos for the Catfish Cove Chronicle. Of course, Leona maneuvered herself into the center of the group, holding her pumpkin and wearing a dazzling smile.

Christy arrived behind the two couples, still dressed in her blood-splattered clothes. She held up her hands for quiet, but someone in the crowd chanted "great costume!"

Finally, the noise subsided enough for Christy to ask, "I'm looking for Kyle Bishop. Are you here Kyle?"

All eyes searched left and right. The back door slammed shut.

Christy pushed her way through the crowd and out the same door that closed moments earlier. Annie squeezed through right behind Christy. She heard tires squeal from the parking lot and saw taillights disappear around the corner, leaving a trail of smashed pumpkins.

"Who was that?" Christy asked Annie. "Who just left in such a hurry?"

Chapter 4

Annie tossed and turned all night. Car taillights flickered in her brain but no details of the car emerged. She awoke to a cold and dreary Saturday morning. Her eyes shot open wide when she felt a warm body pressed against her back.

Then she laughed to herself. Her hand left the warm blankets and patted the body. "When did you join us, you big galoot?"

A tail thumping on the bed answered her pat, and before she could prepare herself, Blue was standing over Annie, licking her face.

"Ewww. Get down! If Christy wasn't tied up with who knows what all night, you wouldn't even be here." Roxy joined Blue in the fun, making Annie pull her pillow over her head.

Both dogs jumped off the bed when Annie's front door opened. She groaned, not ready to communicate with anyone yet.

"Blue, how did you sleep? Are you awake, Annie?" Christy called from somewhere near the front door.

"Now I am. How did you get in?"

Christy laughed. It sounded like it came from the living room. "Your door wasn't locked. Hurry up, I only have a few minutes before I'm heading home to crash."

Annie slid her feet into her sheepskin slippers and wrapped a polar fleece blanket around herself. Christy was sitting on the floor with her back against the couch and Blue draped over her lap.

"You must have missed that dog."

"Yeah, a little. I knew Eddie would take good care of him so he could try to get back into my good graces," Christy said as she stroked the big head. Annie heard Blue groan with pleasure.

"So, what happened yesterday? How did Eddie find you?" Annie added coffee to her coffee maker, dumped in water, and switched it on.

"While I was sitting off to the side waiting for Tyler to finish up, I heard Samantha admit that she led Eddie here to Catfish Cove. I'm not sure if he knew this is where I was living until he arrived."

"Did you know her?" Annie settled into the corner of her couch with Smokey on her lap and Roxy next to her.

Christy shook her head. "Eddie mentioned her name along with some other people he met at bartender school but I never met her. When I saw her in the pub, I never made a connection between her and Eddie. He described her as a bit unhinged and said she was putting the moves on him even though he was married. I think he was trying to make me jealous. I was at the police academy when he did his bartender class and we got married right after I graduated."

Annie got up to pour coffee for the two of them. "Is she a suspect?"

"Definitely, just like I am. Once Tyler let me leave, I talked to people at the Halloween party and—"

Annie interrupted with her eyebrows raised. "Tyler let you question them?"

"He didn't know I went to the pub. I did that on my own. Anyway, no one remembers seeing her even though she was supposed to be working at the bar."

"Maybe she had a costume on and took it off when she brought Blue over." Annie set the two coffee mugs on the coffee table. "Cream and sugar?"

Christy waved her hand. "No, just black. Thanks."

They sipped their coffee in silence for a few minutes.

"I don't think that's what happened." She looked at Annie. "About the costume. I don't think she was wearing one. And even if she was, she still would have been behind the bar serving drinks. Everyone only mentioned seeing the one bartender." She pulled out her notebook. "Dusty Reed? You know him?"

Annie shook her head. "I don't think so. Was he working just for the party?"

Christy stuck her notebook back in her pocket. "Maybe. At any rate, he was not a happy camper having to tend bar by himself." She stood up and stretched. "Thanks for the coffee. I'm heading home for some sleep."

"Why did you drink that coffee if you want to sleep?"

"It won't keep me awake at this point. Come on Blue. I need to introduce you to Bella."

"I forgot about Bella. Good thing you decided not to keep one of her puppies, too, or there wouldn't be any room for you in that ranch house," Annie teased.

"I wanted the black pup. He reminded me of Blue, but Abby and Cody wanted to adopt him when they moved into the Harper House. That's where he belongs."

Annie nodded. "Yeah, he was probably quite attached to that giant fireplace since that's where he was born."

They both laughed and Christy added, "I hope not. Abby doesn't need a puppy bringing all that grime from the front into her brand new apartment in the back of the Harper House. The renovation mess should stay away from her new baby."

Christy walked to the door.

"One more thing I've been wondering about," Annie said. "Why did you agree to meet Eddie alone?"

Christy's head dropped. "I always thought he would change back to the person I had fallen in love with. It's hard to let go sometimes and admit someone will never be what you want them to be."

"Do you have any idea what happened to make him change?"

Christy shrugged and bit her lip. "No. Listen Annie, I know how you got involved in helping to solve the murders that happened here in town, but don't stick your nose in this one. I've got it covered."

"Behind Tyler's back?" she asked with her brow furrowed.

Christy shrugged. "I have to until he decides to let me work with him." She opened the door and passed Jason on his way in as she went out.

"Any coffee left?" He made himself comfy on the couch next to Roxy.

"Yeah." Annie poured the last of the coffee into a mug and handed it to Jason. "Remember how you told me Christy's hiding something about Eddie?"

Jason nodded.

"I think you're right. I can't put my finger on it, but she acted nervous when I asked her why she went to see Eddie alone. And she lectured me to stay out of the investigation."

"Good for her. I couldn't agree more about that." He blew on his coffee before taking a sip. "You won't be taking her advice though, will you?"

"What's that supposed to mean, Jason Hunter? I don't stick my nose where it's not wanted. Stuff finds *me*."

Setting his cup down, Jason placed his hands on both sides of Annie's face. "I'm being selfish. I want you to be safe and stay in one beautiful piece. But don't worry, I always have your back."

They stared at each other before Annie's defenses melted and she let her body nestle into Jason's strong arms. "I'm always careful," she mumbled into his flannel shirt.

Reluctantly pulling away, she said, "I need to get to the café before Leona has a fit. Today is the Halloween brunch, and with the huge turnout for the Halloween party last night at the pub, I expect the Black Cat Café will be mobbed." She carried the empty mugs to the sink and rinsed everything.

"More costumes?"

"Costumes are optional, thank goodness. I'm sure Leona will have her gown on since she loves all that dress up stuff. And I'll bring my crown for her. She swoons over fancy accessories."

"Save me a seat if you can. I'll be by later."

"If the café is too crowded, you can take your food and share it with Camilla in the gallery. She's not too happy to be missing everything, but Martha is helping in the café so Camilla's stuck in the art gallery."

"That's a great idea. She loves hanging out with me." Jason wiggled his eyebrows.

"Hey, none of that." Annie gently swatted Jason's arm. "Don't flirt with that poor girl. She has enough problems reading men without you adding to her confusion." Annie grabbed her warm sweatshirt and quilted tote.

"Do I hear a hint of jealousy?" Jason's lip twitched up slightly.

"Of course not. Camilla isn't your type. You even told me that." Annie flipped her head making her curls fly into his face as he reached to open the door for her.

Jason spun her around, tenderly kissing her. Before he released her to open the door, he said, "Christy is lucky to have you as a friend, but don't forget she's been pulled off the case, so let Tyler use his resources to find Eddie's murderer."

Annie heard everything Jason said, and even what went unsaid. But she had a feeling that Christy was hiding some information about her relationship with Eddie, and that something was putting her in danger. Annie would keep her eyes and ears open. Just in case. Important information had a habit of falling into her lap.

Leona had her favorite oldies station blasting when Annie opened the door of the Black Cat Café. Sweet aromas filled the air along with the music, and unfortunately, Leona's tone-deaf singing clashing with the Beach Boys' harmony. Annie grabbed her favorite lime green apron with jumping black cats and turned the music down a bit.

Leona whirled around. "Hey, that's my favorite song."

The workbench was covered with pumpkin bread, pumpkin scones, pumpkin pies, pumpkin cookies, and Leona's latest creation, pumpkin muffins with chocolate chips and streusel topping. Annie sucked in a deep breath of the delicious smells and grabbed a muffin.

Leona slapped her hand. "No eating until you get the pastry display filled up."

Annie bit into the muffin. "Sure," she answered and laughed, taking a second bite. "These are delicious. You'd better make more. They'll be flying off the pastry shelves today."

Danny pushed the café door open, carrying his Red Sox baseball cap in his hand. "Morning ladies."

Annie wondered how Danny would handle a change in his normal routine of a blueberry muffin, and she took a quick peek at Leona. Leona set a pumpkin muffin on a plate for Danny. "Here's your muffin. Coffee's hot."

He sat at the counter with his coffee and stared at the muffin. "This isn't a blueberry muffin. I can't start my day without one. You know that, Leona."

Leona patted his hand. "Try it. For me. I'm one hundred percent positive you'll love this muffin. Trust me." She fluttered her eyelashes and gave Danny her best sweet smile. "Pleeease?"

He picked up the muffin and sniffed. "Smells good." He set it back on the plate. "Do you have some blueberry muffins in your freezer?"

Leona let out a frustrated sigh. "Yes, but you have to try this one first." She pushed the plate closer to Danny.

Annie covered a smirk, thinking Danny was as stubborn as a three year old.

"Okay." He picked it up again. "Did you two hear about what happened with Kyle last night?" He bit into the muffin.

"Did Christy find him?"

"Uh huh," he mumbled with his mouth full of pumpkin muffin. "Sure did." He continued to eat the muffin.

"And?" Annie sat down next to Danny. "What else did you hear?"

Danny swallowed and sipped his coffee. "He was searching the shoreline from the café right out front here down to the docks on that side." He pointed in the direction closer to the center of town.

"That's where Eddie's body was found," Annie barely managed to say, her eyes wide with surprise.

Chapter 5

Danny finished his muffin and wiped his mouth. "Hey, that was delicious. Can I have another one?"

Leona smiled. Annie laughed. Danny looked at them both with his eyebrows raised.

"Here you go. Another pumpkin muffin. Maybe tomorrow you'll try something else new," Leona teased.

"I doubt it. Not until I'm sick of these." He finished the muffin and used his finger to pick up all the streusel that fell on the plate. "The streusel is the best part and you put that on the blueberry muffins, too. So, I guess I'm sort of eating the same thing still."

Leona shook her head and walked to the oven to take out a fresh batch of muffins. She slid in more trays and set the timer. "Off to keep working at the Harper House?" she asked Danny.

"Yup. I'm loving this project. The upstairs is done and the downstairs is coming along nicely. Abby always invites me into her apartment in the back to see baby Claire when she's awake. She's a beauty, just like her mom."

"I never knew you liked babies," Leona said with surprise in her voice. "Babies make me nervous."

Danny held his arms together as if he was cradling a baby. "There's nothing to it, Leona. And there's nothing more beautiful than a baby asleep in your arms."

Leona looked at Annie. "I'm too old, but you and Jason?"

Annie felt heat rise from her neck into her cheeks. "Geez, Leona. I think you're putting the cart before the horse. We aren't even engaged!"

"I'll have to have a talk with Jason and find out what he's waiting for."

"Talk to me about what?" a deep voice said from the doorway.

Before Annie could tell Leona to keep quiet, Leona blurted out, "Danny loves babies and I thought it would be nice if Annie made us grandparents sometime after we get married."

Jason's face turned a deep shade of pink and he stood motionless with his mouth hanging open.

Annie quickly put a pumpkin muffin on a plate and changed the subject. "Here, try Leona's new muffin. Danny had two."

"I can't stay, but I'll be happy to take it with me. I just wanted to see how things were going before the big rush hits for your Halloween brunch."

Annie bagged the muffin and walked with him out the French doors to the deck. "Sorry about Leona. She doesn't have much of a filter at times."

Jason grinned. "It's a good idea." He kissed Annie's cheek.

"Oh, well, ah, maybe," Annie stuttered, completely flustered. "On another subject, Danny told us that Christy found Kyle searching along the shoreline here last night. What do you think he was looking for?"

"It might be quickest and more accurate to ask Tyler before you come up with a million theories. Just saying." He winked. "I've got to get going. See you later."

Annie watched Jason as he left. His slight limp from a childhood accident was barely noticeable, but his muscular body was impossible to miss under his well-fitting jeans and flannel shirt.

Her heart did a little flip flop with the thought of having a baby. Was marriage and a family in her future, she wondered? The thought made her smile.

Leona had the radio turned up again, but she was quietly humming along instead of drowning out the music with her voice. Mia and Martha arrived together, discussing all the costumes from the party the night before.

"Of course, mine and Harry's were the best. And everyone loooved Charlie. He should have gotten first prize even without a costume," Martha said, loud enough for everyone to hear. "Well, and Leona and Danny too, of course," she quickly added.

Annie couldn't miss the frown on Leona's face. She always had that competitive side and she seemed fine sharing first place with Martha the night before, but now Leona couldn't help but think that Martha felt her costume was the better one. Time for some deflection before Leona had a hissy fit.

"Leona, I think you should wear your gown today for the brunch. You can borrow my crown, too, if you want." Annie reached into her quilted tote bag and held up the crown. "I brought it with me." She raised her eyebrows, waiting for a reply.

Leona smiled. "Great idea. I think I should be the only one in a complete costume since you three will be wearing Martha's beautiful black cat aprons and these witch hats." She pulled the witch hats from her giant canvas bag, handing one to Martha, Mia, and Annie. She fluffed her strawberry blond hair. "And yes, I definitely want to wear the crown."

Annie let her breath out, glancing at Mia and Martha. They both nodded their heads in agreement. Disaster averted.

The women got into a comfortable routine. Annie made pumpkin soup and Leona continued in her frenzy of baking. Mia and Martha decorated the café and readied the tables for the brunch. At ten o'clock, Annie scooted across the hall to check on her Fisher Fine Art Gallery and make sure Camilla was all set for the day.

Annie couldn't contain her laughter when she walked into her gallery and saw Camilla dressed as a French painter, her beret at a jaunty angle atop her newly dyed and straightened black hair. Black cat earrings dangled from her ears and an orange pumpkin was attached to her pierced eyebrow. A baggy, white, button down shirt hung to mid-thigh, cinched with a wide black leather belt. Her shapely legs were covered with black leggings and she towered over Annie in her heels.

With an extravagant bow, Camilla asked, "How may I help you, madam?"

"I'm glad you're in the spirit of the moment," Annie said with a wide smile across her face.

Camilla straightened. "I'm trying, but with all those fantastic smells coming across the hall from the café, I'm feeling a little left out over here." Her lower lip protruded as she lowered her head and peeked at Annie through her long black eyelashes.

"The brunch starts at eleven. As soon as I can, I'll give you a break here and you can get something to eat. How does that sound?"

Camilla rewarded Annie with a smile and a tight hug. "You're the best!"

Annie extricated herself from Camilla's grasp. "Any customers stop in yet?"

Camilla's hand shot out to touch Annie's arm. "Yes. A handsome, sexy guy came in. He said he saw me at the Halloween party last night but didn't have a chance to say hello since he was working."

"How did he find you here?" Annie walked into her office with Camilla following on her high heels.

"He said he asked around at the party. Do you know anything about him, Annie?"

Annie chuckled. "I don't even know who you're talking about, so I can't help you."

She shuffled through some mail on her desk.

"Oh, I'm so scatterbrained sometimes. His name is Dusty Reed." Camilla waited for Annie's reply with her hands folded in her lap.

Annie leaned back in her chair. "No, I don't know him. Wasn't he working as the bartender last night?"

"Yes. That's what he told me. And he wasn't too happy because the other bartender bailed out and he barely had time to take a break. Do you think he's a decent guy?"

Annie shook her head. "Sorry, I heard he was hired for the party. I don't know anything else." Annie stood up. "But be careful, Camilla. Don't jump into something all willy-nilly like you have a habit of doing."

Camilla jumped out of her chair, put her hands on her hips, and waggled her shoulders making the black cat earrings bounce back and forth. "What's that supposed to mean?"

"Well, you know, you fall for a guy at the drop of a handsome dimple and you've been burned." Annie shrugged. "I'm only saying, take it slow. He might be a genuinely decent guy. Is he going to be in town for a while?"

"I think so. He said he was visiting some friends before heading back to someplace or other."

"See, that's what I mean. Pay more attention to the details he gives you. Sometimes they come in handy." Annie threw the empty mail envelopes in the recycling bin and checked her watch. "I'm going back to the café. It's almost time for the brunch to start."

Camilla walked back into the gallery with Annie following.

"By the way, I love your outfit. It's creative and perfectly appropriate for the gallery," Annie said.

Camilla beamed as she ran her fingers through her hair. "I didn't overdo it with the black hair? I'm not sure it works for me."

"Oh no, it works. It makes you look a bit sinister I suppose, but maybe that's not a bad thing with all these men that are attracted to you like a magnet."

Several couples entered the gallery, wandering slowly around and commenting on Annie's photographs and the rest of the show. A new artist in town, Summer Sky, was the featured artist with her hand-dyed fabrics made into beautiful wall hangings and purses. Camilla answered questions about the artist and her work.

Annie took a last look around, proud of herself for bringing her dream of the art gallery to life. When she turned back toward the door, she bumped into Samantha Nichols. Annie grabbed Samantha's arm to help steady her.

"Sorry," Annie said.

"You're exactly who I'm looking for. Do you have a minute?" Samantha whispered, her eyes darting around the gallery.

Annie didn't have a minute but her curiosity won. She checked her watch. "A minute, but that's about it." She led Samantha back through the gallery into her office.

"Have a seat." Annie stood behind her desk and waited for Samantha to get comfortable before settling into her own chair.

Samantha's eyes took in the small room as she twisted her hands together. "You were with Christy last night. When the police chief found Eddie," she said, not a question, but stating what they both knew.

Annie nodded. She squirmed in her chair, trying to be patient. It was killing her, waiting for Samantha to ease into her story, knowing Leona would be furious if she didn't get back to the café, like, five minutes ago. She wanted to hit Samantha with a million questions, but she bit her tongue.

"You're probably wondering why I had Eddie's dog." She didn't meet Annie's gaze, her eyes fixated on her lap. "Eddie contacted me about a month ago. Ya know, just a friendly email. We've kept in touch ever since we met at bartender school." She finally looked up at Annie.

"Right. Did you know Christy too?" Annie asked, even though Samantha and Christy said they didn't know each other when they met the night before.

She shook her head. "I never met her. Eddie told me about her, but he said he liked to keep his worlds separate. Ya know . . . keep the bartending people separate from his and Christy's friends." She stood up and walked to the bookshelves and pulled out one of Annie's books. "Are you a photographer?"

"Listen, Samantha. I'd love to hear what you're trying to find the nerve to tell me, and I don't think it has anything to do with photography." She stood up and walked to the door of the office. "I have to leave. How about we meet later when I'm not so pressed for time?"

Samantha's hand shot out and took hold of Annie's arm. "Wait. I feel terrible. I'm the reason Eddie came here to Catfish Cove."

Annie's nerves jumped into high gear. "What do you mean?"

"I told him Christy was living here." She finally met Annie's stare with fear-filled eyes. "He wouldn't be dead if he hadn't come to Catfish Cove."

Chapter 6

Annie checked her watch again. It was a quarter to eleven. She sent a text to Leona saying she would be there as soon as possible.

"You knew they weren't together anymore?" Annie asked.

"Oh yeah. Eddie called me the night Christy left him. He was brokenhearted. A complete basket case. When I saw the article in the Catfish Cove Chronicle about her getting hired here, I let Eddie know." Samantha rubbed the back of her neck. "Do you think Christy killed him?"

"Why would you say something like that?" Annie certainly wasn't planning to give Samantha any information. Her goal was to get whatever she could out of Samantha. Any background details she could provide about Eddie might come in useful.

Samantha shrugged. "Eddie said Christy stole some of his stuff when she left Cape Cod. That's why he wouldn't give Blue back to her. I think he came here to make a swap."

A big red flag flew across Annie's brain. She suspected Christy was hiding something about her past with Eddie and Annie was pretty darn sure Christy wasn't planning to share this tidbit of information with her.

"And Eddie asked you to bring Blue to the parking lot? Why didn't he just bring Blue himself?"

"He didn't explain that, but my guess is he wanted to be sure Christy brought whatever it was he wanted back. Her being a detective and all made him feel like she had the upper hand."

Annie's phone beeped with a new text message, which she ignored for the moment. "Why are you telling me this?"

"Like I said, with Christy being the detective, she might just sweep some evidence under the rug or plant evidence on someone else."

"Like you?"

Samantha nodded. "I'm worried. Someone has to look at the situation from Eddie's perspective, too. Will you do that?"

Annie held up her hands. "Wait a minute. I'm not involved in this investigation."

Samantha's eyes turned hard and cold as she stared at Annie.

Annie looked away. "Okay. I'll do what I can."

Samantha gave the tiniest of nods and left the office, never looking back.

Annie leaned on her desk for a minute, trying to organize her thoughts and make sense of what Samantha told her. Annie had no connection to Eddie Crank or Samantha Nichols, but she had developed a friendship with Christy. She certainly didn't want to jeopardize that fragile relationship but she couldn't turn a blind eye if Christy figured out a way to deflect evidence away from herself.

And what about Tyler as police chief? He and Christy had a romance starting; would he be swayed by his personal feelings for Christy? Annie shook her head.

Camilla poked her head around the doorway. "You okay?"

"I'm not sure." Annie's phone beeped again with another text. "But I need to get to the café before Leona sends the cavalry out to find me."

Camilla put her hand out to stop Annie as Annie hurried past to get to the café. "Listen. Something was odd about that girl. I know I'm not the best judge of men—well, you've made me realize I'm closer to the worst judge of men—but I can read women. That girl had an agenda. Don't let her bully you into something you don't like."

Annie paused. "You weren't even in the office with us. How did you pick up on that?"

Camilla rolled her eyes. "Let's just say it's my gift. Trust me on this, Annie. Don't be too naïve. She wants something from you."

"Thanks. Gotta run." Annie trotted from the gallery as her phone beeped again. She didn't have to look at the message to know Leona was losing her patience.

A line was forming at the door of the Black Cat Café. Annie had to endure nasty stares as she maneuvered past everyone and let herself in. The door smacked into Leona as she reached to open the door from the inside.

"Whoops, sorry about that." Annie smoothed Leona's lime green gown and straightened the crown that was threatening to topple off her strawberry blond hair.

"Where have you been? I've sent you a hundred text messages," Leona said through her clenched teeth.

"Uh, I'm here now so let's get this show on the road." Annie deflected Leona's frustrated question. "Wow, the cafe looks fantastic."

Martha was putting the finishing touches on the pumpkins. Some were carved with lights inside and others were filling in as vases for beautiful yellow, purple, and orange fall flowers. Mia was on the deck adding more carved pumpkins to the railing and on top of hay bales.

Leona grabbed Annie's arm. "What's going on?"

"I'll tell you later." She tilted her head toward the door and smiled. "People are waiting to come in. Open the door and be the hostess with the mostest." She forced her face into a broad smile, hoping it looked genuine to Leona.

Leona frowned at Annie but replaced her grimace with a smile and a huge welcome when she pulled the door open. "Come on in. We have so many Halloween treats for you today."

Witches and clowns, beggars and cowgirls, soccer players and cheerleaders all shuffled their way into the café. Leona had all the drinks on one cart—coffee, tea, hot cider and a spicy pumpkin latte with a bowl of whipped cream for topping. Another cart had Annie's pumpkin soup and a turkey pumpkin chili. The pastry case was overflowing with spicy pumpkin muffins— iced or plain—pumpkin scones with cranberries, pumpkin shaped sugar cookies decorated like jack-o-lanterns, chocolate chip pumpkin bread, and pumpkin pie. Leona even had homemade pumpkin ice cream to go with the pie. From the grill,

Leona offered pumpkin pancakes with maple syrup.

The booths and counter stools filled quickly and more people waited for a place to sit or took their treats to go. It was a hectic, crazy rush of customers, keeping the four women on their toes until around one o'clock when the crush died down.

Annie refilled the pastry case, wondering how many muffins she had handled that morning. When she straightened, she faced Tyler Johnson, bringing back all the memories of Eddie's murder and the odd conversation she had earlier with Samantha.

"Tyler, I hope you're not too hungry, we're sold out of some of the sweet treats."

"How about a muffin? Do you have time to sit with me for a minute?"

Annie wiped her forehead with her sleeve and looked around the café. Mia wasn't busy so Annie asked her to take care of the pastry case. She put a muffin on a plate for Tyler and a slice of pumpkin pie with homemade pumpkin ice cream on a second plate for herself.

He sat gazing out the window, tapping his fingers on the table. Annie set the plates down. "I'm having a spicy pumpkin latte, do you want one, too?"

Tyler looked at her as if he had forgotten where he was. "A what?"

"Spicy pumpkin latte with whipped cream. It's good."

Tyler's lips turned down at the edges. "No thanks, black coffee works for me." His head turned back to the window.

Annie slid into the booth opposite Tyler after setting down the two mugs. She followed his gaze and realized he was looking toward the spot where they had found Eddie the night before. In the sunshine, everything appeared normal as usual. The water lapped against the shoreline. A few boats bobbed on Heron Lake. A young couple walked along the sand hand-in-hand.

Annie reached across the table, touching Tyler's hand. "You're lost in thought. What's going on?"

"Hmmm?" He picked up his mug and sipped the steamy coffee. "Oh, this murder has me puzzled."

"How so?" Annie stuck a piece of pie covered with ice cream into her mouth. She pushed her plate toward Tyler. "You should try this. It's delicious. Well, the muffins are fantastic, too, but take a bite of the pie with some ice cream. You look like you need a distraction."

Finally, Tyler focused on Annie. "That's an understatement. Just when I thought my love life was going in the right direction." He shook his head.

"What's going on with Christy?" Annie kept her voice light but her stomach dropped with concern for her friend.

"I wish I knew. Things were going great yesterday with the costume stuff. Especially when she tricked you with her fake injuries. But ever since I heard the name Eddie Crank, she changed. She'll barely talk to me now that I took her off the investigation. I wish I could work with her to solve this murder. People in town get kind of edgy if they think there's a killer on the loose." He took a bite of Annie's pie. "Did you make this?"

Annie smiled. "Not sure if I made this exact pie but it is my recipe. What do you think?"

He nodded his head as he stole another forkful. "You can finish it." Annie pushed the plate in front of Tyler. "Any idea what's going on with Christy?"

"No. She's always on her phone but hangs up as soon as she sees me. What do you think? You always have feelings about this sort of stuff. I need someone to bounce some ideas off of and Christy is avoiding me."

Annie looked around the café. "You're right. I do have a funny feeling about Christy, but I don't want to talk about it here. Can you meet me after two? That's when we're closing."

"Yeah." He slid off the seat. "I'll be back."

"Tyler? I think Christy might be in some sort of danger. Try to keep an eye on her."

Chapter 7

The café was emptying out. Finally. It had
been a successful brunch but way too
hectic as far as Annie was concerned.

Leona busied herself cleaning the grill and
work areas. Mia scrubbed all the tables,
and Martha chatted with the last few
departing customers.

"Any food left for a starving fan?" Annie
heard a familiar voice, and her heart
quickened. Jason leaned over the pastry
display. "Are you hiding from me,
sweetheart?"

Annie straightened and arched her back,
twisting from side to side, working the
kinks out from all the bending in and out of
the shelves while serving customers. "And
if I am?"

He patted his pocket. "You won't get this
surprise I have for you."

Annie's face broke into a big smile. "You do know how to lay on the charm, Mr. Hunter. How about I trade you something delicious for a peek at the surprise?"

"Hmmm. What are you trading?"

She leaned close to Jason and whispered, "Me."

His eyebrows shot up and his eyes popped into huge round spheres. "It's a deal. And I'm getting the better half of this bargain. I'll be waiting at the booth by the window over there." He tilted his head to the booth farthest from everyone.

Annie cut a double piece of pumpkin pie, added a healthy scoop of pumpkin ice cream and a spoonful of whipped cream for good measure. She carried it to the booth, sliding in across from Jason. Their knees met under the table, sending tingles through her body.

"Looks delicious," he said, staring at Annie. His eyes never left her face as he shoveled a forkful of pie into his mouth. "The pie is good, too." He grinned as his knee rubbed against hers and she felt a calmness settle into her core.

"It's been a hectic morning."

Jason nodded as he continued to enjoy the pumpkin pie.

"First, I had to deal with Christy at my apartment when she picked Blue up, then Samantha found me when I was checking on Camilla at the gallery."

Jason held a finger up. "About Camilla. I did visit her earlier but she was swamped with customers. I hope you have some food left to bring over."

Annie slapped her forehead. "Oh dear, she's going to be mad at me. I promised I'd give her a break but I never had a chance. Maybe I'll bring her something now. Okay?"

"I guess so, but hurry back."

Annie threw some pumpkin muffins in a bag and poured a big pumpkin latte for Camilla. Mia was finished cleaning tables so Annie begged her to bring the food and drink over.

"Are you avoiding Camilla?" Mia asked.

"Yeah, sort of. She's going to be starving and mad. Do you mind?"

Mia took the bag. "Not at all. I'm glad to get out of the café for a few minutes and see something else."

Annie slid back into the seat across from Jason.

He looked up in surprise. "That was quick."

"I begged my mom to bring it over. So, where were we?" She pressed her knee against Jason's again and smiled.

He swallowed the last bite of pie. "You were telling me about Samantha."

"This is interesting." Annie rested one elbow on the table with her chin nestled between her thumb and forefinger. "Samantha is afraid Christy will target her as the murderer."

"Maybe she *is* the murderer. She knew Eddie would be meeting Christy. No one remembers seeing her at the pub when she was supposed to be working. Did she tell you where she was?"

Annie shook her head. "Actually, I didn't even think to ask. She acted so upset and felt guilty for telling Eddie that Christy was here in town. She thinks if she hadn't told him, he would still be alive."

A shadow fell over Annie and Jason. "Am I interrupting or do you have time to talk now, Annie?"

Jason's hand covered Annie's in a possessive gesture.

Annie glanced at her watch. "I didn't realize what time it is. Yeah, Tyler, I'll meet you in the parking lot."

Jason's eyebrows raised questioningly after Tyler left the café. "What's this about?"

"Sorry. Tyler was in earlier. Christy isn't talking to him and he asked for my opinion on what might be going on. I told him I'd have time to talk once the brunch was over." Annie slid from the booth. "Dinner tonight? Just you and me?"

"And my surprise. Don't forget what you promised to trade," Jason said trying to keep a straight face.

"No worries." Annie told Leona she had to leave, but everything was well under control.

Tyler was pacing in front of Annie's car when she caught up to him. "How about you follow me to the police station and we can talk in my office," Tyler suggested.

"Will Christy be there? She might think we're conspiring against her if she's not included."

"Good point. She might be. She said she had to finish up some paperwork in her office. Your apartment instead?"

Annie thought for a minute. It was far from ideal, but unless Christy saw Tyler's car parked in the driveway, they could talk without interruption. Or suspicion. "Okay. Follow me." They drove the short distance back to Cobblestone Cottage.

Annie opened the door to her apartment and Tyler followed her inside. Roxy was all over Tyler hoping for a cookie, but he didn't carry any in his pocket like Jason always did. She gave up and settled back on the couch.

Annie turned on her teakettle. "Want some tea?"

"Okay." Tyler sat at the table, hands folded together, his foot jiggling up and down. "Do you believe Christy's story about Eddie lunging at her and she was defending herself?"

"You don't?" Annie asked with a shocked tone.

He scratched his head. "I don't know what to believe. Christy is so jumpy whenever I try to discuss it with her. I know she wants to be back on the investigation but I just can't do that yet."

Annie poured the tea and brought it to the table. "Samantha told me something. I don't know if it's true or not, but she said Christy stole something from Eddie when she left him and he came back here to try to get it back. Blue was the bargaining chip. Samantha's afraid Christy is going to pin the murder on her. You need to find out more about that story."

Tyler finally focused. He took out his pad and scribbled some notes. "Anything else?"

"Start with the Mixed Drink Bartender School where Eddie met Samantha. Find out who else was in that class with them. Christy told me Eddie changed after their honeymoon. I think something happened while she was finishing up at the police academy and he was doing the bartending thing."

Tyler nodded his head as he scribbled more notes. "Thanks, Annie. This is just what I needed to move forward. Christy really had my mind all locked up. I couldn't think straight."

Tyler stood up, his tea untouched. "Will you let me know if you hear anything else?"

"Of course. And Tyler?"

He looked at her, waiting.

"I think Christy's in some kind of danger. If she didn't kill Eddie, someone else did. You have to figure out who."

"And what if Christy's the killer?" Tyler asked.

"Well, you have to find out why. Maybe it *was* self-defense like she implied."

Tyler sucked in a deep breath. "This will be in the papers tomorrow anyway. Eddie didn't die from stab wounds."

Annie's hand stopped with her teacup halfway to her mouth.

"He lost a lot of blood from the stab wounds, but it looks like he died when his head smashed into a rock."

"Are you sure?"

"Yes. We found a blood covered rock on the cement wall near his body."

Annie replied in barely more than a whisper, "Did someone bash his head or did he fall?

Tyler shrugged. "Not sure yet. But we suspect someone helped him to the spot where he died."

Chapter 8

Annie called Roxy and they followed Tyler out the door. "Are you doing any extra security for the trick-or-treaters around town tonight?" Annie asked.

"Everyone in the department will be working extra hours. We'll have lots of visibility for traffic problems and any pranks from teenagers. Is the Black Cat Café handing out treats?"

"Of course. Leona is making caramel covered apples for all the kids that show up at the ice cream window. And peanut butter pumpkin dog treats for any canine trick-or-treaters. I think we'll be the last stop for many, so they can enjoy the apple treat right there on the deck. And we'll be selling Leona's pumpkin ice cream with or without hot fudge sauce."

"Save an apple for me. That was my favorite as a kid."

Annie smiled. "Will do." She turned left toward the lake with Roxy, and Tyler drove out in his cruiser.

"What do you think, Roxy? Any chance Christy is the killer?"

Roxy lifted her head to stare at Annie as her tail waved back and forth.

"No. I don't think so either. She is hiding something though." They followed the Lake Trail, Annie, lost in her thoughts, and Roxy, lost in the smells.

Suddenly, Roxy ran to the edge of the water and grabbed a piece of fabric. Annie tried to see what Roxy had, but her dog thought they were playing a game of chase and easily evaded Annie's attempts to get the material. Eventually, Roxy lost interest and darted off after a new scent, dropping her treasure.

Annie picked it up by two corners, watching water drip to the ground. Stenciled in white on the heavy dark blue fabric was the logo and name, Catfish Cove Pub. How did it get way down here?

Annie watched the direction of the waves lapping on the shoreline. She wondered if someone lost it near where Eddie was found dead and it drifted to this spot. She remembered Danny saying that Kyle was found searching for something the night before. Was it Kyle's apron?

Annie pushed her fingers into the pockets of the apron but both were empty. She flipped it over. The initials KB were written in black permanent marker. Kyle Bishop?

"Come on Roxy. We need to go make a surprise visit."

Annie and Roxy pulled into Christy's driveway and parked behind her SUV. The curtains were closed over the windows of her tidy ranch. Closed before it was dark? That couldn't be a good sign.

Annie knocked on the front door. Silence. She knocked again. Louder and called,

"Christy, are you home?" Finally, the door opened. Christy's hair was down around her face, uncombed, and she looked like her world was shattered.

"Hey," Christy said with no enthusiasm. "Come on in." She turned around, leaving Annie to follow or not.

Roxy barged past Christy, wagging her tail and sniffing Bella and Blue. The three dogs were like long lost buddies and they ignored the tension between Annie and Christy.

Christy slumped onto her sofa. "Tyler refuses to let me help with Eddie's murder investigation. He probably thinks I'm the murderer," she stated, her eyes glazed over, no emotion in her voice.

"Did he say that?" Annie sat opposite Christy. "That he thinks you're the murderer?"

"No. He didn't have to. I could feel his stare through my back when I went to the station." She finally raised her eyes to meet Annie's. "I can't just sit around, I'll go crazy. I have to do something."

Annie chose her words carefully. "Did you know any of Eddie's friends? Interests? Anyone who would want him dead?"

"Besides me?" Christy snorted with disgust.

Annie leaned forward, placing her hands on Christy's knees. "Listen, if there's anything else you can think of, this is the time to tell Tyler. Without more background information, he doesn't know where to look. What about Samantha?"

Christy stood up, hands in her pockets, and stood in front of the window, staring at closed curtains instead of her garden. Her soft voice broke the silence. "Believe me, I'm wracking my brain trying to come up with something." She whirled around. "This is what I trained for, finding clues, following clues, putting clues together." One hand raked through her hair. "My thoughts keep coming back to his time at that bartender school. Something must have happened then, while I was finishing at the police academy. Samantha is a link for sure, but I don't know how."

"Who else?"

"I told him to invite his new friends over, but Eddie said he liked to keep his worlds separate." She snorted. "That's kind of strange, don't you think?"

Annie shrugged. "And then you went on your honeymoon?"

"Yup. He got a couple of phone calls that he told me were connected to job searches. Then we got home and nothing was ever the same again."

"Did he—" Annie began but was interrupted by someone banging on the door.

The three dogs barked at the closed door. Bella jumped up on it with her front feet.

"Christy. I know you're in there. Open the door."

Christy's eyes opened wide. She pulled an envelope from her pocket and stuffed it into Annie's hands. "Take this. Don't look inside unless something happens to me. Go out the back door." She pushed Annie through the kitchen, grabbing her gun and holster off the counter. "Don't go to your car until I let him in."

"Do you know who it is?"

"I think so. It could lead to something important." She held Annie's arm for a few seconds. "Be careful."

Me be careful, Annie thought. Christy needed to be careful. Whoever was at the door wanted something from her.

Annie tucked the envelope into the inside pocket of her jacket. What was she safeguarding for Christy? Annie's fingers itched to look inside. Not now. She had to safely get to her car.

Annie inched around the side of Christy's house, glad for the shrubs she could hide behind. A dark sedan had her blocked in. Great. She couldn't leave. Annie texted Tyler. *Come to Christy's house. Now.*

Almost immediately, he texted back. *On my way.*

With her heart racing and threatening to pop right through her chest, Annie inched as close to a window as possible. It was closed, blocking the voices, but she could just see through a small crack in the curtain. Dusty stood inside the door, his arms waving around and his finger jabbing at Christy. Roxy sat quietly but alert next to Annie.

"What is Dusty doing here?" Annie whispered to Roxy.

Annie saw Christy's fingers tighten around her gun. Dusty put his hands up as he backed away from her, stopping when he hit against the door.

Was she going to shoot him? *Hurry up Tyler*, Annie silently said, as she looked toward the road. We don't need another body.

Annie held her breath, listening as hard as possible. Christy's high-pitched voice just barely made it through the closed window. "I told you not to come here. Someone will figure out the connection."

Annie flipped around to rest against the house. Dusty? How did Christy know Dusty? This was getting weirder and weirder.

Finally. She heard tires crunch in the driveway. Tyler's cruiser pulled in next to the dark sedan. He should be blocking that car in. Oh well.

Annie waved to Tyler and rushed to join him as he walked to the door.

With his hand raised ready to knock, the door opened. Dusty stepped backward, bumping into Tyler's strong chest.

Annie, standing behind Tyler, saw a startled expression cross Christy's face before it settled into a neutral appearance.

"Mr. Reed is just leaving, right?" Her eyes bored holes into Dusty's forehead.

"Yes, sorry to bother you."

Annie waited for Tyler to grab Dusty and demand to know what was going on. She watched in shock as he let Dusty return to his car and drive off.

Tyler took a step, uninvited, into Christy's house. Annie rushed in behind him with Roxy at her heels. She had no idea what Tyler's plan was, but she decided she could intervene if it got ugly.

Christy stood blocking their entrance so they couldn't move beyond the mat inside the door. Annie looked down and smiled to herself. She was standing on the image of a black lab, Christy's soft spot, the way into her confidence.

"What do you want Tyler?" Christy growled.

"An explanation. What was Dusty doing here?"

"It's personal, and if I'm not mistaken, it's not a crime to have a personal life." She stood with her hands on her hips and her legs spread apart. Even though Tyler's height dwarfed Christy, her posture said 'don't mess with me.'

"No, it's not a crime. Can't we sit down and discuss this?"

Annie held her breath again. She desperately wanted to help Christy, but Christy had to work with them. Unless she was hiding something awful.

Annie stuck her hand in her jacket pocket and remembered the envelope inside. She wouldn't discuss this in front of Tyler unless Christy brought it up.

Christy sighed and stepped back. "Okay, come in. Annie, close the door behind you."

They all settled in Christy's living room. No one wanted to start the conversation, so Annie cleared her throat and made a big assumption. "How do you know Dusty?"

Christy's shoulders slumped. "I don't really know him. He was at the bartender school with Eddie and Samantha. I never met either Dusty or Samantha, but I heard the names mentioned."

"Why did he come to your house?" Tyler asked.

"He wanted to know what Eddie and I talked about last night when I met him. Eddie came to town looking for me, to warn me that I was in danger, but he's the one that got killed. It doesn't make any sense to me."

"How did he find you here?"

"You heard the same thing I heard last night. Samantha told him I was here. She said she never met me before, and that's true, but she's seen me around town. Eddie told me Samantha was going to teach me a lesson."

Tyler leaned forward with his elbows on his knees. "What kind of lesson?"

Christy rubbed her thighs with her hands. Her lips puckered into a grimace. "Eddie finally figured out that I wasn't the problem, but his other friends, Samantha, Dusty, Kyle and Dennis were dragging him down. He came to apologize to me and beg me to go back with him."

"And?"

"When I told him, 'no freaking way,' he lunged at me with his knife." She shrugged. "And now he's dead, so it doesn't matter, does it?"

Chapter 9

Tyler stood up and paced across the small living room, his hands pushed deep into his pockets, his jaw clenched.

Christy patted Blue who sat leaning against her leg. "Now I'm thinking Eddie drove me away on purpose to get me away from his friends." She shook her head. "What a dope he was. I could have helped him with the mess he got into, but no, his ego wouldn't let him do that."

"Any idea what the mess was?"

"Some scheme they all got involved with." She pointed to Annie. "It's all in the envelope I gave you before—all that I know, which isn't much. I just wanted to be sure someone looked in the right direction if something happened to me."

Tyler turned around and put his hand on Christy's shoulder. "I'd like you back on the case. With one condition."

Christy's eyes were suspicious. "What's your condition? I don't like to work that way."

"I know, but in this case it's for your own good. You have to work behind the scenes. No interviewing suspects. I'll do that and fill you in. I'll follow all the leads. Agreed?"

She nodded. "Agreed. But I have a condition, too."

The edges of Tyler's mouth turned down but he waited for her to continue.

"I want Annie to be a sounding board. Sort of a consultant." Christy's left eyebrow arched, her head tilted, and her gaze shifted between Annie and Tyler.

"That works." He grinned. "She always pokes her nose in anyway, even when we don't want her to."

"Hey! With that attitude, I'll just stay at the café and make a gazillion pumpkin pies." She pretended to be offended. "Oh, and by the way, I found something interesting before I came here. It's in my car. But you two probably don't give a hoot about it."

"Of course we're interested," both Tyler and Christy blurted out at the same time.

They all walked outside. Annie noticed Christy's eyes dart around as if she was checking the street and perimeter of her property. Maybe it was second nature for her, but Annie sensed Christy was feeling more vulnerable than usual. Having the two dogs with her would help.

Annie reached into the back of her car and picked up the soggy apron. Holding it up so the other two could read the Catfish Cove Pub lettering, she watched as they both shrugged dismissively.

"So? Anyone could have lost it," Tyler said.

Annie turned it over, showing the initials in black.

Christy's hand snatched the apron. "KB—Kyle Bishop. I found him wandering the shoreline last night. He wouldn't tell me what he was looking for. He just laughed at me. A kind of evil laugh. I'm going to start my internet search into his background."

Tyler frowned. "You weren't supposed to be doing any investigating last night."

Christy shrugged. "It wasn't police work, just my personal thing."

Tyler shook his head. "I was afraid I wouldn't be able to stop you. And just so you know, since you'll be working in the background, I'm not taking you off the suspect list. I think it's best if everyone still thinks the focus is on you. Are you okay with that?"

Christy smiled. "Yeah. Keep those four thinking they're off the hook. Samantha, Kyle, Dennis, and Dusty. It's got to be one of them."

Tyler headed to his cruiser. "My first stop is to the little cottage Eddie was renting after he moved out of Samantha and Kyle's place. We searched last night but I want to have another look around. Oh, I'll drop his laptop off here with you, Christy. See if you can find some interesting leads."

"I didn't know you had his computer." Her face became serious.

"Right. I didn't tell you before because I didn't know your connection." He smiled at her. "I'm glad you let your defenses down enough to trust me."

"Fair enough. You had to be sure about me. If I were you last night, I would have assumed I was the murderer, too." Christy pretended to stab Tyler with an invisible knife. "Watch out." She wiggled her eyebrows. "I could still be fooling you."

Annie and Tyler both laughed. "Welcome back to our world, Christy. I like you much better this way," Tyler said. He took a step toward her with his arms spread as if he was planning to hug her. He abruptly stopped.

"I know you have to pretend we're not on the same team." Christy scowled. "Come back later and we can pick up where we left off, you know, before I met Eddie last night."

Annie opened the back door of her car for Roxy to jump in before she slid into the front seat. "I'm out of here since I didn't agree to chaperone you two, just provide my excellent sleuthing skills."

Tyler tried to keep a serious expression on his face as he pointed his finger at Christy. "I'll deal with you later." He lowered his voice. "If anyone is listening they can take that any way they want to."

Christy held her hand out to Annie. "You can give me the envelope back. I feel safer now."

Annie pulled it out, wishing Christy had forgotten. She still wanted to know what it said with her own eyes, in case Christy left anything out. Not that Annie felt Christy was the murderer, but she still might be hiding some information that she wanted to follow on her own. And that would put Christy in danger with no one having her back.

Christy stuck the envelope in her jacket pocket and whistled for her two dogs, telling them, "Come on. Let's get to work."

Annie backed out and headed to the Black Cat Café.

Leona had her oldies station on and dozens of caramel apples lined up on the counter. They looked like little soldiers with their wooden handles sticking up. Annie snuck up behind her and poked her fingers into Leona's sides.

"Hey!" she exclaimed. "Now look what you've done."

Leona had been piping chocolate over the dipped apples and the last line was all crooked.

"I'll take that one for Tyler. He wanted me to save one for him." Annie set the rejected apple on a plate off to one side.

"Tyler? What about Jason? You'd better set two aside." Leona added a second apple to the plate.

"These are beautiful. Have you thought about adding them to the menu?" Annie asked.

"Good idea. It could be a seasonal offering." She straightened. "I hope I have enough for tonight. What do you think?"

"There are plenty of pumpkin shaped sugar cookies. You could offer those if the apples disappear too quickly. Do you want me to make some more sugar cookies, just in case?"

Leona threw her an apron. "Yes, please."

Annie set the apron on the counter. "First, I need to check in with Camilla. She's going to be chomping at the bit for a break unless Martha showed up."

Annie popped a pumpkin shaped sugar cookie, with orange frosting and chocolate chip eyes, in her mouth and grabbed a couple more for Camilla.

She pushed into the gallery, happy to see several customers wandering around. Camilla was off to one side, facing Annie, talking to someone. The man turned around to see what distracted Camilla. It was Dusty Reed.

Annie winked at Camilla and thought to herself that it didn't take Dusty long to make another appearance in the gallery. Was he genuinely interested in Camilla, or was he fishing for information?

Annie stood to one side, listening to the conversations of the customers. She loved to hear feedback about her photographs, and she was especially proud of her late fall display. She had captured beautiful shots of the foliage around Catfish Cove, including colorful reflections on the lake. Reflections always fascinated her. Her favorite in this show was a clump of birch trees dressed in their golden yellow foliage with the stunning reds and oranges of the maples in the background. The whole scene was a mirror image on the perfectly still water of Heron Lake.

"Excuse me, I have a couple of questions," a young woman said, interrupting Annie's thoughts.

"Oh, of course."

"Are you the photographer?"

"Yes." Annie smiled.

"Your camera takes lovely shots."

"Excuse me? My camera?" Annie tried to hide her annoyance, but the camera didn't take the shots without Annie's expertise behind the lens.

"Yes, well, *you* take amazing photos, I should have said." She blushed slightly. "I'm traveling through town, and I want to come back earlier next year during foliage season. I don't want to miss seeing it for real."

"Early October is a good time to plan on visiting."

"Thanks."

She moved back to her group of friends, leaving a sour taste in Annie's mouth. She knew the woman didn't mean anything by her comment, and the camera certainly helped, but Annie spent years working on taking the perfect shot. She considered the lighting, the angle, and most important, the way she composed the subject in the frame. She didn't use any software to manipulate her shots. She wanted to find the perfect photo with her own talent.

"You look annoyed," Camilla said.

Annie waved her hand, dismissing the comment and her bad feeling. "It's nothing."

"Can I take a break now?"

"Yes." She leaned close to Camilla. "What's up with your new Romeo?"

Camilla's eyes twinkled. "Dusty is handsome, isn't he? He wants to take me out for dinner tonight. Should I go with him?"

Annie hesitated. "Sure, but stay around people and see if you can pump him for any information about Eddie."

"Are you serious? Could he be the killer?"

Annie shrugged. "He could be, so be careful."

Chapter 10

When Camilla returned from her break, Annie told her to check in if she found out anything interesting on her date with Dusty. "Do your flirty thing tonight, it always works."

Camilla stuck her chest out and wiggled her shoulders. "Like this?" she asked with her head dipped down and her eyes peeking through her long lashes.

Annie laughed. "You've got it down to a science, my dear. Stop at the café after your dinner if you want to sample one of Leona's caramel apples. Or her pumpkin ice cream."

By the time Annie returned to the café, Mia was hard at work wrapping the finished caramel apples in clear bags and tying them with orange ribbons.

"Beautiful," Annie said, picking up one of the wrapped treats. "The kids are getting quite the delicacy tonight. You'll have to do this every year, you know."

Leona looked up. "I like traditions. Are you going to stay and help hand them out?"

"Of course. That's what I enjoy the most about Halloween; seeing all the kids dressed in their costumes. I'm hoping to take some photos, too. Kids are one of my favorite subjects." Annie got out a mixing bowl to start the cookies.

"Huh, kids keep popping up into the conversation around here," Leona teased with a twinkle in her eye. "What costume are you going to surprise the kids with tonight? You have to get dressed up if you want to help," Leona told Annie.

"Really?" She thought for a moment. "I'll dress as a farmer—overalls, mud boots, and a straw hat. That goes with the apple theme."

"All right. I have a witch costume complete with a black wig and a green wart on my nose."

"Geez Leona, you'll scare the little kids half to death."

"You think so? I'm a kind witch. I made all these yummy caramel covered apples for them," Leona said, looking puzzled.

"We'll see, but be prepared for some tears," Annie warned. She measured all the ingredients into the bowl and turned the mixer on. The twirling beaters calmed her. Once the dough was perfect, she popped the bowl in the refrigerator to cool for a half hour. "These are going to be the best cookies ever!" Annie announced.

"Did you taste the batter?"

"Ah. Don't tell anyone." They laughed.

While the dough chilled, Annie texted Tyler. *Your caramel apple is waiting for you. If you have time, stop in at the café.*

The café door opened and Tyler walked in checking his phone. "Great timing. Can you sit with me for a few minutes?"

"Yup. The sugar cookie dough is chilling. I'll bring the caramel apple over." Annie picked up the apple with the squiggly chocolate, saving the perfect one to take to Jason later.

"Here you go," she said as she set the plate in front of Tyler. Annie slid into the seat opposite.

Tyler picked up the apple and studied the chocolate decoration. "What happened here? Was Leona drunk when she decorated this one?"

"No. I scared her and she nearly jumped out of her skin."

Tyler took a big bite. Apple juice sprayed across the table. "These are kind of messy. You better have some wipes available for the kids."

Annie filed the suggestion away for later. "So, Tyler, what do you think about Christy's story?"

One eyebrow arched up as Tyler looked at Annie over his apple. "Story? You don't believe her?"

"Do you?"

"Yes and no. I think she knows more than she's sharing."

Annie leaned forward. "I agree. And that envelope she gave me but took back? I wish there had been time for me to look at what was inside."

"I dropped Eddie's laptop off at Christy's house." Another bite, and the apple was three quarters gone.

"I hope you looked at it first. There could be something really important to your investigation on it."

He nodded his head. "I copied the hard drive so I can check up on anything Christy tells me about."

"You don't trust her?" Annie's eyes widened.

He set the last bit of apple on the plate. "Here's the thing. I like Christy. I want to believe her and trust her, but the cop in me is sending up red flags. I've learned to pay attention to those warnings even when I prefer to ignore them."

"It must be hard to balance those two views."

Tyler nodded and finished the apple. "I'm going to her house when I'm off duty tonight, after the kids are done trick-or-treating." He tried to wipe some caramel off the edge of his mouth but the napkin stuck and made a bigger mess.

Annie laughed. "You're right about these apples being a big mess. The kids can walk to the lake and rinse off there."

"Are you serving anything else later?"

"Pumpkin shaped sugar cookies and pumpkin ice cream." Annie slid from the booth. "I need to get the cookies cut out. The dough should be chilled by now. Tyler?" She waited until she had his attention. "Keep me up to date with the information from Eddie's laptop, okay?"

Tyler nodded. "I'll share what I can." He stood up, ready to leave.

"I like Christy, too, and there's something going on that makes me nervous. I can't get what Samantha told me about Christy stealing from Eddie out of my head. We have to find out first if it's true, and if it is, what did she steal?"

"I'm digging into a couple of leads from his computer but I'm not sharing that with Christy. Not yet, at least."

Annie took the dirty plate to the sink and got her bowl of dough from the refrigerator. Since no one was watching her, she broke off a small chunk of dough and popped it in her mouth. She preferred the cookie dough to the final product and could never resist a taste. It was perfect.

With some flour on the counter top, she rolled her dough and cut out dozens of pumpkin shaped cookies. When those were all on the cooking trays, she found her cat cookie cutter and used that one for the second batch. After all, the Black Cat Café should have cat sugar cookies.

She slid the trays in the oven and set the timer. She had just enough time to mix up the frosting—orange frosting and chocolate chip eyes for the pumpkins; black frosting and orange collars and green eyes for the cats. Decorating was always Annie's favorite part. It got her creative juices flowing, just like when she had her camera in her hands.

All the caramel apples were packed and arranged on serving trays for the trick-or-treaters, so Leona and Mia helped frost the cookies when they were cool enough.

Leona wiped her hands on her apron. "There. That should do it. I picked up some bags of candy too, just in case. Now, I'm heading home to change. Be back at five thirty. The parade down Main Street is first, so I don't expect any kids here until six at the earliest."

Annie got a text from Christy. *I found something weird. Can you stop by?*

She answered, *just finished at the café, will be there ASAP.*

What now, Annie wondered. Something on Eddie's computer? She threw a few cookies in a bag for Christy and left with Roxy.

Christy was waiting outside when Annie pulled into her driveway. "This way." She headed away from her house to the yard across the street.

"Blue disappeared earlier and I heard him barking from over here. This house has been deserted ever since I moved in. Look how completely overgrown the yard is." Christy led Annie through a gate swinging on one hinge. "He kept barking, but I couldn't find him until I got down on my hands and knees and crawled through this tunnel in the weeds."

Annie followed Christy, hoping she wouldn't put her hand down on a snake or some other slimy object. The tunnel opened into a space about three feet in diameter.

Christy leaned against a tree as she gazed across the street with a direct view of her house. "What do you think?" She pulled her legs up, making room for Annie.

"This is where you found Blue?" Annie asked as she swiveled her head around taking in the complete view.

"Yup."

"Do you think Blue followed someone's scent?"

"That's exactly what I think. I think Eddie was spying on me."

"Why?" Annie felt the hairs on her neck rise. Being spied on was about the creepiest thing she could imagine. Well, besides someone actually invading her space inside her home.

"That's what I have to figure out, and I'm hoping his computer gives me some clues."

Annie brushed the dirt and grass off her hands. Something else was stuck there. "Ick. I put my hand in someone's chewed gum. Gross."

Christy pulled it off Annie's hand and smelled it. "Mint. Eddie always chewed mint gum."

Annie backed out of the tunnel, following Roxy and being extra careful where she placed her hands. She straightened and cracked her back. "That's really strange if you ask me."

"Uh huh. I'm going to keep an eye on this spot to see if any other scumbag crawls in."

Chapter 11

The drive back to her apartment didn't take Annie long. The bag of cookies for Christy was still on her car seat. Absentmindedly, she munched on one. She hoped Jason had some overalls she could borrow. Her own mud boots would work and she was pretty sure she had an old straw hat somewhere in a closet. If she couldn't find it, she'd call her mother to bring one to the café.

Annie brought the caramel apple she saved for Jason and headed to his house first. She was starting to be quite comfortable there and spent less and less time in her own apartment. Jason was happy about that development.

"I brought you a treat," Annie called when she stepped inside.

Jason clumped down the stairs, rewarding Annie with a beaming smile. "You're all the treat I need." He hugged her and gave Roxy a dog bone. "Do you have time to sit down or are you on another mission of madness?"

"I can sit for a bit." She handed Jason the caramel apple. "You can save it for later if you want to. It's pretty messy to eat."

"I'll save it." He set it on his counter and walked with Annie to the couch. "What have you been up to?"

"Well, baking sugar cookies for the trick-or-treaters tonight." She left out her visit to Christy's house with the odd tunnel and viewing spot across the street from her house. No need for Jason to worry about her more than normal. "Leona insists I wear a costume. Do you have overalls I could borrow?"

"Overalls? What kind of costume is that?"

"I'm going to be an apple farmer. You know, the girl that grew the apples for the caramel apples Leona slaved over all day." She tilted her head, waiting for his reaction.

"What should I dress as? An apple tree?" The corners of Jason's eyes crinkled as he tried to keep his mouth in a serious expression.

"Are you going to help at the café tonight?"

"Sure. That sounds like fun. I need to keep an eye on you so I can make sure you come back here with me for dinner." He grinned. "I don't want you to slip away from the promise you made to me in exchange for my surprise."

Annie settled deeper into Jason's comfy couch, leaning inside his warm arm. Thinking about what his surprise could be made her want to skip the parade on Main Street and handing out caramel apples to the trick-or-treaters. She wanted to jump right to dinner. And the rest of the evening.

He tightened his arm around Annie. "You're smiling. Care to share your thoughts?"

"Huh? Oh, nothing. You'll need a costume or Leona won't let you help."

"Hmmm. How about I wear my chef's hat and apron?"

"That's funny. You don't even know how to cook."

He pouted. "I make a mean salad, and I'm sure I'll be a super duper ice cream scooper." Jason stood up and checked the time. "Let's get this show on the road, it's already five o'clock."

He returned with denim-striped overalls that two of Annie could fit in, but, whatever, it was a costume. She rolled up the legs, stuck her feet into her polka dot mud boots and pulled the straw hat she found in the top of Jason's coat closet over her curls.

Fanning her arms out to her sides, she twirled around. "How do I look?"

Jason caught her after two spins. "Good enough to eat." He pretended to munch on her neck but she squealed and pulled away, laughing.

As they headed out the door, Annie's phone chirped with a new text message from Christy. *I think someone's in the tunnel. Can you come over?*

She thought quickly and told Jason she would meet him at the café.

"No way. I know you, someone will convince you they need help and I won't see you for hours. We're driving together."

"Okay but I have to make a stop at Christy's house."

His eyes narrowed. "Why?"

Annie grabbed his hand. "I'll explain in the car."

Jason insisted on driving. Annie filled him in about the tunnel and Eddie stalking Christy. "At least that's the theory," she added.

He turned his head to stare at her, obviously annoyed. "And you were going to tell me about this, when?"

She shrugged. "It may be nothing."

"And Christy might be making all this up and she could be the killer. Annie, don't be so trusting."

They drove in silence until Jason pulled in behind Christy's SUV. He reached over and squeezed her hand. She smiled, glad he cared enough to worry about her. Annie pointed across the street to the abandoned house and explained where the tunnel was before they got out of Jason's car. From Christy's yard, the tunnel was completely invisible.

The curtains were partly opened. Annie saw Christy pace back and forth in her living room as they walked to her front door.

Annie heard Blue and Bella barking. Christy opened the door before Annie had a chance to knock. Christy pulled her inside, almost slamming the door on Jason, who was a few paces behind.

"Why did you bring Jason? I wanted you to come alone," Christy said without concealing her annoyance.

"Well, he's here because we were on our way to the Halloween parade in town. I can leave if you want." Annie challenged Christy with her words.

"No, it's all right. I'm wound up pretty tightly and he caught me by surprise." She picked up her flashlight. "Come on. Let's take a look. I haven't seen anyone leave yet."

Christy led them out the back door with the flashlight off. Annie felt Jason's hand on her tense shoulder, which was a tiny bit reassuring. All this cloak and dagger stuff was beginning to unnerve her, especially with the branches creaking around her, creating shadows everywhere she looked.

Christy walked silently through her backyard to the edge of her property before crossing the street. No cars were in sight. No people. No nothing for that matter. The broken gate hung open enough so they could squeeze through without moving it.

Christy crouched as low as possible. Annie and Jason followed her lead. At the entrance of the tunnel, she got on her hands and knees, finally turning on her flashlight and moving forward quickly.

They reached the opening. Empty.

"How did they get out?" Christy whispered. "There must be another path." As her head swiveled around following her beam of light, Annie gasped.

"Look. In your house. Someone's inside." Annie pointed to a figure moving in front of Christy's living room window. The same window Annie had watched Christy pace in front of.

They heard a door slam, but no one appeared.

Christy crawled at top speed back through the tunnel. "They must have gone out the back door. But where are the dogs?" She flew across the road, her feet barely touching the pavement, flinging her front door open. Bella and Blue were happily gnawing on marrowbones without a care in the world.

Christy threw her flashlight across the room, letting it shatter into pieces on the floor. "I've been duped. One of us should have stayed in the house. Whoever was inside knew exactly how to get by my dogs." She walked into her kitchen and shrieked. "Eddie's computer is gone. They stole his computer."

Annie saw a small leather-bound book on the table but Christy quickly moved it into a drawer, which also contained the envelope Christy had given Annie earlier. Her curiosity soared but she filed the information away for another time. Now she needed to focus on what Christy found on Eddie's computer.

"Did you discover anything useful yet?" Annie asked.

"His passwords were saved so I could log into his email and several other sites. From what I've gathered so far, he had something going on with Samantha."

"What kind of something? Romantic?"

"Samantha was pushing for that, but I think Eddie was only stringing her along so she would help him find me."

"That doesn't make sense. If Samantha was interested in Eddie, and Eddie wanted to get back together with you, why would Samantha tell Eddie you're living here? She would want to keep Eddie as far away from you as possible."

Christy rolled her eyes. "Samantha didn't know Eddie wanted to get back together with me. He kept that a secret from her so he could manipulate her. Of course, Eddie was the master at manipulating everyone to get what he wanted. Only, it didn't work on me this last time."

Christy's theory sounded fishy to Annie. Maybe Eddie and Samantha were working together to find Christy and get back whatever it was that she allegedly stole from Eddie.

Annie shook her head. The scenario changed depending on who was telling the story.

Christy had her phone out. "I need to call Tyler. Have him search for Samantha. My guess is she's the one who stole Eddie's computer. She knows Blue and he wouldn't mind if she came in my house. And with a couple of marrowbones, she'd be able to keep Blue and Bella happy while she searched."

Annie's nerves tingled. Samantha told Annie she suspected Christy would pin

Eddie's murder on her. What was going on? Who was lying?

Chapter 12

Christy threw her phone to join the flashlight that was smashed on the floor and balled her hands into fists. "Tyler said I have to stay here. Keep a low profile. He's heading to the Catfish Cove Pub, hoping to find Samantha and ask her some questions." She paced like a raging cougar. "I can't stand this having to stay behind the scenes stuff."

Annie ignored the drama, not letting it distract her from getting to the bottom of whatever was going on. Christy was acting like she had already decided Samantha was guilty of Eddie's murder without any concrete evidence.

Annie glanced at Christy's desk. She wondered how she could manage to see what was in the envelope and the leather-bound book that had been hurriedly pushed out of sight in Christy's desk drawer.

Jason, who had remained quiet in the background, touched Annie's arm. "Let's go to the pub. Maybe we can accidentally, on purpose, bump into Samantha." He shrugged. "Who knows, maybe she'll tell you something useful. It would be helpful to find out what she's been doing for the last hour or two."

Christy spun around. "Great idea. Be sure to text me any information you get." She plopped down at her desk and opened her laptop. "I have enough information from the history on Eddie's computer to do some more searching from mine, even without his passwords."

She took a long drink from her mug before focusing on her screen while Annie and Jason let themselves out.

"What do you make of Christy's behavior?" Annie asked Jason.

"You know her better than I do." He opened the door for Annie before scooting around to get into the driver's side. "Is she always so hysterical and impulsive? With her background as a detective, I would expect her to be more thoughtful and deliberate with her actions."

"Exactly what I was thinking. She certainly isn't acting like herself, nor what I have come to expect to be her cool, calculated behavior. Either Eddie threw her for a loop, or she's panicking and trying to cover her tracks by throwing us down the wrong path."

"What do you mean?" Jason turned quickly to look at Annie.

"Samantha told me she was afraid Christy would try to pin Eddie's murder on her." As Jason drove toward town, Annie watched the scenery go by without really seeing it. "Why did Samantha show up so soon after we found Eddie's body? And why wasn't she at work last night at the pub like she was supposed to be? She has some explaining to do, that's for sure."

"Don't jump to any conclusions. She may have a perfectly reasonable explanation." Jason stopped his car so some kids dressed in Halloween costumes could run across the street.

"Someone stole the computer. If it wasn't Samantha, who was it?" Annie finally turned her head to look at Jason.

Jason backed into a parking spot down the street from the pub. "Who else in town even knew Eddie besides Samantha and Christy?"

Annie counted off on her fingers. "Kyle Bishop, the cook at the Catfish Cove Pub; Dusty, the bartender at the Halloween party; and maybe Dennis, the owner of the pub. I'm not sure about Dennis."

Jason held Annie's arm, preventing her from opening her car door. "Do they have any reason to kill Eddie?"

Annie puckered her lips. "That's what someone needs to find out. The common thread seems to be when Eddie went to bartender school. Something happened when Christy was finishing at the police academy and Eddie met those other clowns at bartender school."

Jason released Annie's arm. "Let's see if we can find out anything from Samantha. She was helping Eddie with Blue, so maybe he was closest to her."

The pub was busy for Halloween happy hour. Jason and Annie wove their way through the crowd while reading the happy hour drink menu on the blackboard above the bar.

"Want me to get you one of those?" Jason asked, pointing to the Poison Punch. He leaned close to Annie's ear. "Appropriate for Halloween and the event that happened yesterday, don't you think?"

Annie's head swiveled around to Jason. "That's not funny! Someone was murdered." Her mouth formed an 'O.' "I wonder if Tyler ever checked the body for poison."

"Of course he would. The autopsy would reveal anything like that." Jason steered her to the end of the bar where Samantha sat nursing a drink.

"Hey, got a minute?" Annie asked as she slid into the seat next to Samantha, and Jason sat on her other side.

Samantha didn't turn her head. Her shoulders slumped over the counter and her head sagged. "Sure. I've already been grilled by Catfish Cove's finest. What do *you* want? My break's over in about five minutes."

"What are you drinking? We'll have the same."

"Poison Punch." Samantha nodded her head to get Dennis's attention, pointed to her drink, and put up two fingers.

"Interesting name. What's in it?" Annie asked.

Samantha handed Annie her glass. "Try it. Mine's a virgin since I'm working but yours will have red wine, apple cider, and boysenberry juice, with apple slices for a garnish."

"Did you say poisonberry?" Annie asked with a crease forming between her eyebrows.

"Ha." Samantha's lip actually twitched slightly. "No. I said boysenberry but I like poisonberry much better. I know a few people I'd serve *that* to. Starting with that annoying detective."

Annie sipped the drink. "This is delicious. Try it, Jason." Samantha's comments registered in Annie's brain, triggering several questions, but she decided not to voice them. Yet.

Dennis slid two glasses to the end of the bar, expertly timing the push so they stopped in front of Samantha. She slid one to her left and one to her right. "Enjoy," she mumbled without looking at either Annie or Jason.

"So, have you been here working all afternoon?" Annie casually asked before picking up her drink.

Samantha's eyes narrowed. "Is that your clever way to ask if I'm the one who stole Eddie's computer?"

Annie felt her face heat up and was glad of the low lighting to hide her embarrassment. "I suppose so."

"Didn't I tell you," Samantha's voice rose full of annoyance, "that Christy would try to point evidence in my direction? Maybe *she* hid the computer *herself*."

"No, I saw someone in her house when we were across the street." Annie sipped some more Poison Punch and licked her top lip.

"In that tunnel in front of the abandoned house?"

"You know about it?" Annie tried to keep her voice calm and nonjudgmental.

"Sure. Eddie told me he was spying on Christy. Trying to figure out how to get his stuff back."

"What stuff?" Annie asked, staring directly at Samantha. "You need to give me something. I can tell the Police Chief to start looking in a new direction."

"Right. He's infatuated with Christy. What good will *that* do?"

Annie tilted her head. "You have to trust me on this."

Samantha bowed her head, her lips pressed tightly together. She swiveled her bar stool to face Annie directly. "Here's the thing. When we were all at school together, we did some stuff and made some money. Eddie stashed it until we could get together to split it up. That never happened, because it disappeared the same time Christy ran."

"Why didn't Eddie go to the police?"

She turned away from Annie. "Ha, it was kind of complicated. Going to the police would have been more trouble than tracking down Christy. Besides, she is the police."

"How much money?"

"Plenty, but that's all I'm sharing for now. You've got to give me something before I tell you more." Samantha slid off the barstool and walked behind the counter without another glance at Annie or Jason.

"Wait," Annie shouted over the din in the pub.

Samantha slowed and came back to stand across from Annie.

"How did you end up here?"

"I met Kyle at a party and he invited me to come back with him; said there was a job opening for a bartender here. I was completely surprised to find out Dennis was looking for a bartender. He hired me on the spot since he knew me from school. He was my teacher."

"And then Christy moved here. What a coincidence," Annie added.

"You could say that. A lucky break for us."

"Why didn't you just try to get the money back and leave Eddie out of the equation?"

Samantha glanced over her shoulder at Dennis who had been keeping an eye on her the whole time. She leaned close to Annie. "Dennis and Kyle wanted to do that. They were furious when Eddie showed up here at the Catfish Cove Pub." She lowered her voice. "And even angrier when they found out I was the one who told Eddie that Christy was working here as a detective."

A rowdy customer banged his empty beer mug on the bar and Samantha hustled over to get him a refill.

Jason slid onto the stool that Samantha had vacated. He put his arm around Annie, pulling her close so he could whisper in her ear. "Interesting."

Annie finished her Poison Punch and shivered. "This drink gives me the creeps. Do you think the police missed something about Eddie's cause of death?"

"You think he was poisoned?" Jason asked, a crease forming between his brows.

"This might sound farfetched, but what if he didn't lunge at Christy, but was actually falling into her and she misread his action. Her stabs didn't kill him. The real murderer was watching, moved him near the water to make it look like he cracked his head on a rock or something like that to cover up that he had poison in his system."

Annie felt her skin crawl when she realized she was being watched.

"Do you want a refill of your Poison Punch?" Dennis asked, his jaws grinding together. "You already wasted enough of Samantha's time. Either order or make room for someone else to sit here."

His dark eyes stared into Annie, making her squirm and look away. Jason threw a twenty-dollar bill on the counter. "Keep the change," he said as he put his hand on Annie's back and guided her out of the pub.

Chapter 13

Once outside, Annie filled her lungs with the cold, crisp air. "Something is off with that guy. It felt like he was looking right inside my head, reading my thoughts." She wrapped her arms around herself, trying to ward off the chill from Dennis's stare.

Costumed kids with parents trying to keep up streamed toward the Cove's Corner parking lot. Goblins, ghosts, witches, cowboys, cowgirls, and kids in every other costume imaginable carried their empty bags in anticipation of receiving lots of sweets.

Martha and Harry sat in Harry's antique black Ford with orange streamers attached, waiting to lead the Halloween parade down Main Street. Charlie, Harry's parrot, perched in his cage in the back seat and squawked greetings as kids walked by the car.

Charlie was always a hit at events and had become the town's unofficial mascot. Annie could hear his squawking and laughed when something appropriate rang out. She assumed Harry had worked on getting Charlie to say boo and trick-or-treat. Half the time, Charlie got the timing and phrase right, causing the kids or their parents to jump in surprise then laugh when they saw Charlie sitting in his cage.

Jason held Annie's arm, guiding her toward the Black Cat Café. "Let's leave the car parked on Main Street. No point in trying to find another spot now with the parade about to start."

They walked quickly away from the pub trying to avoid any collisions. Annie turned her face for a second to ask Jason a question when a tall, muscular man bumped into her side, almost knocking her to the ground.

"So sorry." He caught her right arm and Jason steadied her left side. "That was all my fault. I'm late for a date."

"You're the bartender that's been helping out at the pub, right? Dusty Reed?" Annie asked.

He held his hand out. "Yes, and you are?"

Annie shook his strong hand. "Annie Fisher. How long have you been in town?" Annie felt a slight tug from Jason but she dug her heels in, determined to find out more about this guy.

"Not long. The owner of the pub, Dennis Franchino, asked me to help out through this busy time."

Annie held onto Dusty's hand so he couldn't leave. "Did you know Eddie Crank?"

Dusty's gaze darted between Annie and Jason. "Why all the questions?" He pulled his hand from Annie's grasp and took a step away from her but her hand darted out and held his arm.

"Why did you go to Christy's house?" she demanded to know, staring into his intense green eyes.

Dusty leaned into Annie's face and she jerked backward. "She has something I want." He held her gaze before spinning on his heels and hustling toward the pub.

"Geez, Annie," Jason said. "Now he'll have you in his crosshairs along with the rest of that gang working at the pub."

"What do you mean?"

"Come on, Annie," Jason said with frustration lacing his voice. "Samantha told you she's worried about Christy throwing suspicion for Eddie's murder in her direction. Samantha and Kyle are living together. Now, this Dusty creep says the owner of the pub asked him to come to town to help out right after Eddie showed up? Don't you think they might all be connected to Eddie's murder somehow?"

Annie shrugged. "Maybe." She started walking without looking at Jason. She could feel his eyes boring into her. Waiting.

"You should tell all this to Tyler."

Annie's mud boots clomped on the sidewalk.

"I already told him that Samantha said Christy stole something from Eddie when she left and that's why he came to town. To try to trade her dog Blue, for whatever it was she stole."

Jason let out a long breath of air. "Of course you would tell him before you told me." Jason stopped walking. "I'm not feeling up to helping scoop ice cream. I'm going back to my house. Can you get a ride home?"

Harry's car slowly made its way down Main Street with Charlie squawking trick-or-treat over and over. The happy babble of kids following the car drifted toward Annie's ears but she didn't even notice.

"I'll find a ride home," she finally said in barely a whisper. She quickly wiped a tear from her cheek so Jason wouldn't see, even though he was already walking in the opposite direction, back to his car.

Annie watched him disappear into the crowd, mentally kicking herself for being such a fool. She didn't want Jason to worry about her. That was the only reason she didn't share every detail, she told herself. Of course he would think she still had feelings for Tyler.

The high school marching band followed behind the trick-or-treaters. The leader was dressed in a clown costume, prancing and waving her baton to the beat of the big drums. It should have made Annie feel nostalgic and happy with her memories of being younger and marching down main street all those years ago, but all she felt was an emptiness—a small lonely island in the middle of the noise, music and laughter.

She felt an arm around her shoulder, startling her out of her funk. "Why aren't you at the café helping Leona?" She heard Camilla's cheery voice.

"I'm on my way," Annie answered as she noticed Camilla was not alone.

Camilla introduced Annie to Dusty Reed, unaware of the fact that Annie and Dusty had met only minutes earlier.

Dusty nodded his head, but said nothing. Annie forced a smile.

Camilla chattered away, walking between Annie and Dusty as they all headed to the Black Cat Café. When Camilla paused to breathe, Dusty said to Annie, "This is quite a Halloween event here in your quaint little town."

"Yes, it is. We tend to do all the holidays up into something special. Halloween is one of my favorites. Except this year," she added.

"Oh, why is that?" Camilla asked, almost jogging on her high heels to keep up with Annie's quick pace.

Annie glanced at Camilla, then Dusty. "Ah, you know. The other night?"

Camilla's hand went to her mouth. "Oh, wasn't that just awful? That poor guy murdered by the lake. He wasn't even from around here. Now, who would do something like that?"

Annie felt her mouth twitch up slightly. Leave it to Camilla to put all the cards right out there on the table. "Yes. Exactly what I was thinking, Camilla. Who would do something like that?" She leaned forward to look in front of Camilla toward Dusty. "What do you think about this tragedy?"

His mouth opened, closed, and opened again. "I don't know," he managed to stutter in response.

Camilla jabbed him in the side with her elbow. "Aw, come on Dusty, you told me you came here because of Eddie. You wanted to have a beer with him but he was already dead. Or something like that."

"That's interesting, Dusty," Annie said. "And what were you two going to chit chat about?"

Dusty reached to open the door of the café, stepping back so Annie and Camilla could enter first. "Just old times when we were at the Mixed Drinks Bartender School together. I did see him sitting at the bar, but we never got a chance to talk."

Leona glared at Annie as she entered the café. Her angry face, plus her warty nose and witch hat, made Annie pause. Leona threw an apron to Annie. "It's about time you showed up. Where's Jason? I thought he was going to help too."

"Something came up. Are you here alone?" Annie looked around at all the caramel apples lined up on the counter, trays of cookies covered with plastic, and the ice cream cooler humming.

"Your mother isn't feeling well, Danny had to work late at the Harper House and, well, Martha is tooting around with Harry in the parade. Yeah, I'm alone."

Camilla, still in her painter outfit from earlier in the day, grabbed a couple of aprons. "We can help."

Leona looked at Camilla as if she was seeing her for the first time, then smiled at the handsome face behind her. "And who do you have with you, Camilla?"

"Oh, this is Dusty. We were stopping here for some ice cream, but we can pitch in if you want us to." She looked at Dusty. "Is that okay with you?"

He shrugged, obviously not sure what he was getting himself involved in but wanting to please Camilla.

"Okay then. You two scoop the ice cream while Annie and I hand out the caramel apples and sugar cookies." She gave Dusty a once over with her eyes. "Not bad, but you need a costume to fit in with the rest of us." She handed Dusty a witch hat. "This will have to do."

Kids began to stream through the door as soon as Annie pulled her straw hat over her strawberry blond curls. Leona cackled and held a caramel apple toward a young girl dressed like a princess. She wouldn't take the treat.

Annie bent down to the girl's eye-level and whispered in her ear. The little girl smiled and let Annie hand her the treat.

"Nice one, farmer girl," Leona said and winked at Annie. "You definitely have the touch with kids."

Leona stopped cackling and instead pasted a friendly smile on her face. Costumed kids stared at the caramel apples with big round eyes, carefully carrying their treat to sit outside at a table with their parents. A long line was forming at the ice cream window, keeping Camilla and Dusty busy.

Annie's initial negative feeling toward Dusty was melting slightly as she watched him work easily with Camilla. He smiled at her often and acted comfortable around her and the customers. Had she misjudged him earlier?

The next face that appeared in the window shocked Annie. Christy reached in and tapped Dusty on the arm. Annie saw his jaw clench and he gave a slight, almost imperceptible shake of his head. Christy frowned. What was she doing at the ice cream window?

Chapter 14

Annie snuck a cookie for herself before she pushed the tray closer to Leona. "I'll be right back." She ignored Leona's protest and headed outside to find Christy.

The tables were full with parents eating ice cream and kids getting sticky from their caramel apples. What a mess. Annie found Christy hunched over the railing, gazing out at the lake.

"Couldn't stand it in your house any longer?" Annie asked, standing next to Christy.

Christy's lip puckered up on one side. "That's an understatement. I'm used to being on the go all the time. I wore a path on the hardwood floor with all the pacing back and forth. The dogs even gave up on me taking them outside for a walk."

Without turning to face Christy, Annie asked, "So, what's going on with you and Dusty Reed?"

"Nothing," Christy said but her voice hesitated.

"I don't believe you. Is he stalking you? Harassing you?"

Christy turned to face Annie and grabbed both of Annie's arms, snarling between clenched teeth. "Listen, and listen carefully. You don't want to get involved in this. I told you before; I've got it covered. Now, butt out! For your own good."

Annie's mouth fell open and she shook Christy's hands off her arms. "You just answered that question whether you realize it or not. Now tell me this—is Camilla in danger by dating him?"

"What? Tell Camilla to stay as far away as possible." Christy returned to her lake-gazing position but Annie saw her jaw muscles clenching and unclenching rapidly.

Back in the café, Leona was on the last tray of caramel apples and Annie could tell she was having trouble keeping up the friendly chatter with the kids.

"Take a break, I'll finish here," Annie told Leona.

"Thanks." Leona lifted her witch hat and ran her fingers through her hair. "I didn't expect this to be more tiring than serving the regular customers. I'm beat. Hey," she elbowed Annie in the side. "What's the story with Camilla and her hot date?"

Annie shrugged. "I'm not sure. He's part of the group that knew Eddie, and he showed up at Christy's house. Christy just about bit my head off when I asked her about him." Annie watched Camilla and Dusty bump and jostle each other as they scooped the last of the ice cream.

"He looks harmless enough," Leona said. "Unless being too handsome is a risk factor."

"Who's too handsome?" a voice asked behind Leona.

Annie laughed and watched some red creep up Leona's neck. "Hey Danny, nice timing. Leona was just telling me that baby Claire is smitten with your handsome face." Annie said, covering for Leona.

Leona laughed nervously. "Yep. I don't like having any competition but I guess I could think about sharing you with that adorable baby girl."

Danny took one of the last caramel apples off the tray and looped his arm through Leona's. "Join me outside, my sexy witch?"

Only a couple of kids were still waiting for a treat. A little girl dressed in jeans and cowboy boots with blond curls spilling from under a cowboy hat several sizes too big, and a boy a couple of years older, wearing a blue shirt with a badge pinned on his chest.

"Where's your pony?" Annie asked the little girl.

"He's tied up outside. Can I take an apple for him, too?"

Annie's eyes widened. "Really? Your pony's outside? I'd love to see him."

The adorable girl slipped her tiny hand into Annie's hand. "Come on. His name is Amigo. My name's Sally." She looked up at Annie with dark blue eyes. "Amigo means friend. He's my best friend. Do you have a best friend?"

Annie nodded. "Yes, I do as a matter of fact. Her name is Roxy . . . my dog." Annie realized it was only partly true what she told Sally. Roxy was her best four-legged friend, but Jason was her true best friend and she had to fix what she broke earlier. Of course, Jason had every right to be upset, even angry that Annie shared more with Tyler about what was going on with Christy than she told Jason.

Annie picked up the last caramel apple, set the empty tray down on the counter and followed the cowgirl outside to a table with a young couple, but no pony.

"Mommy, she brought out an apple for Amigo."

Sally's mom rolled her eyes and smiled sheepishly at Annie. Sally picked up a stuffed pony at least half as big as she was. She hugged him to her chest, whispered something in his ear and then handed him to Annie.

Annie squatted down to Sally's level. She gently accepted Amigo and stroked his soft covering.

"He's the most beautiful pony I've ever seen," Annie told Sally. Her eyes lit up like the fourth of July. "I think this apple might be too sweet for him, though. Maybe your mom or dad would like to have it."

"Okay," Sally said and handed the apple to her mom. "Amigo already ate tonight anyway."

Annie felt the corners of her mouth twitch up but managed to stay serious. "Yes, too much food and Amigo might get a tummy ache." Annie handed Amigo back to Sally. "Thank you so much for introducing us. He sure is special."

Sally's mom silently mouthed a 'thank you' to Annie as Sally climbed into her lap.

"Next time you come to the café, you can meet my dog, Roxy. He likes cowgirls."

Sally rested her head against her mom's shoulder and clutched Amigo tightly. "Does Roxy like ponies?"

Annie patted Sally's head. "Of course he does."

Annie said goodbye and hustled back into the café. No more kids, but Tyler was helping himself to a handful of orange frosted sugar pumpkin cookies.

"Hey! Those are for the trick-or-treaters," Annie scolded.

"I'm in my costume," Tyler sputtered with crumbs flying in every direction. After he swallowed and brushed the stray crumbs from the corner of his mouth, he continued, "What's Christy doing here?"

"Cabin fever. Big time. She almost bit my head off earlier."

Tyler's forehead creased. "Any particular reason?"

Annie busied herself cleaning up the empty trays and motioned for Tyler to follow her to the sink. With her voice low she said, "I asked her about Dusty Reed since Camilla's out with him tonight."

"And?"

"And, I got nothing but a big earful to back off and tell Camilla to stay as far away from him as possible."

"Interesting. I've been doing some background checks and I can't find a thing about Dusty Reed. He was a late signup for the Mixed Drinks Bartender School class that Eddie was enrolled in, but no information before that."

Annie finished rinsing the trays. "Do you think it's a false identity?"

"That's my first assumption. But why? What could he be hiding?"

"Is there any information on the disk from Eddie's computer?" Annie leaned against the sink waiting for Tyler's response.

"I wasn't going to tell you this but," Tyler crunched his lips together, "here's the thing. I put a tracking device on Eddie's computer. Just in case."

Annie's eyes widened.

"It's still in Christy's house."

"That can't be," Annie said, shaking her head to reinforce her puzzlement. "I saw someone in Christy's house. Jason was with us too."

"You may have seen someone, but that person didn't take the computer."

"Are you going to tell Christy about this?"

Tyler looked away. "This is so hard. I like Christy, but I have to put my job and the safety of the community first. She needs to tell me why she staged the theft. I want her to start sharing information with me, but so far, she's been a closed book. Not just closed, but slammed shut and locked inside a big vault."

"Huh. This makes no sense." Annie looked outside and watched Dusty and Camilla standing close together at the railing, not too far from Christy. "Maybe Camilla can get information from Dusty. She's good at that."

Annie pulled Tyler outside. "Camilla, thanks for helping out tonight. Did you try the pumpkin ice cream?"

Camilla quickly pulled her hand from Dusty's. "It was hard not to." She sucked on her bottom lip. "Yup, delicious."

Annie noticed Christy keeping her eyes on Dusty during the conversation. She moved slightly to block Christy's view. If Christy wanted to be part of the conversation, she could join them; otherwise, as far as Annie was concerned, *Christy* could butt out.

"How long will you be in town, Dusty?" Annie asked, putting her arm on Camilla's shoulder.

In typical Camilla fashion, she started to jabber all the information she had already pulled from Dusty. "Oh, he's working on a project and just loves Catfish Cove. Right, Dusty?" She continued without giving him any time to respond. "He's staying for as long as needed. And he was fortunate to know the owner of the Catfish Cove Pub and fills in as bartender when needed." Camilla looked at Dusty through her long lashes.

"Interesting," Annie said, tilting her head to one side. "Tyler and I would love to hear what sort of project it is."

Dusty looked between Annie and Tyler. "Well—" he started, but was interrupted before he could say anything more.

"You need to come with me," Christy grabbed Dusty's arm and pulled him away from the others.

"What the heck?" Camilla said, staring at the disappearing backside of her date. She dug around in her big purse. "At least he gave me his cell phone number. It's in here somewhere."

Camilla pulled out a business card triumphantly. "Ta-da. He's getting a piece of my mind for leaving me stranded here."

Tyler held his hand out. "Can I look at the card he gave you before you call him?"

"Sure." Camilla handed Tyler the card with Dusty's handwritten phone number.

Tyler flipped it over. "Huh, this might be some help in figuring out who this Dusty Reed is." Tyler held the card up so Annie and Camilla could read the name. Dusty R. Pearson had been hastily crossed out, but was still legible.

"Oh shoot, I've been duped again," Camilla said and hit the side of her head with her open palm.

"All of us, Camilla," Tyler added. "I'm going to do some more searching."

Chapter 15

Camilla gave Annie a ride back to her apartment after she made Tyler promise to let her know if he found out anything more about Dusty—or whoever he might actually be.

She walked by Jason's car, wondering if she should go to her apartment or his house. The light from his windows looked warm and inviting. First, she'd take Roxy for a walk and then decide if she was ready to tackle the mess she made with Jason.

No Roxy.

Annie panicked and raced across the driveway, storming into Jason's house, out of breath and wild-eyed.

Roxy jumped off the couch at the sound of the door opening and greeted Annie. "I was so worried when you weren't in the apartment." She crouched down and hugged her best four-legged friend.

"I thought she was lonely, so I took her for a walk, fed her, and kept her over here. I hope you don't mind," Jason said with one hand on Annie's head, letting his finger twirl in a curl.

Annie stood up and sobbed into his chest. "I'm so sorry I didn't tell you everything that was going on with Christy."

He held her tight. "It's okay. Come and sit down. Dinner will be ready soon."

"You still made dinner for me? I thought you were angry."

"I was, but I realized that your stubbornness is one of the things I love about you. It's good and bad, but it's you." His lips twitched and his eyes sparkled. "And, you made me a promise that I intend to keep."

Annie pushed him away playfully. "Well, Mr. Hunter, I hope it's a special meal or I might not keep that promise."

"Oh, I'm not worried about that."

He turned Annie around and she gasped. His table was set with a beautiful royal blue tablecloth with silver candlestick holders and white candles burning. Two places were set with white square porcelain plates and freshly polished silverware. An orange pumpkin sat in the middle, filled with white lilies.

"I hope you brought your appetite."

Annie's stomach growled at the thought of food. She looked down at her ridiculous outfit as an apple farmer. "I want to change first."

"Perfect. That gives me just enough time for one last detail."

Annie's heart flipped and flopped. How could she have ever considered messing up her relationship with this considerate man?

"I'll be right back." Her comfy, worn-in jeans and soft as puppy fur flannel shirt were still hanging in Jason's downstairs bathroom where she changed earlier. Annie took a quick look in the mirror as she finger-combed her curls. She gave a shrug and returned to his living room.

A pop made her jump, but it was only champagne.

"I guess this is a special meal," she said and smiled.

Jason grinned and filled two champagne flutes. Handing one glass to Annie, he clinked her glass. "To us." After they both took a sip, Jason set his glass down and a small box magically appeared in his hand. He flipped the top open and held the velvet box toward Annie. "Will you marry me?"

Her hand went to her heart and Jason grabbed the champagne flute before it slipped to the floor.

"Of course." Annie's eyes narrowed slightly. "Did Leona put you up to this?"

Jason choked. "Leona? Why would you say that?"

Annie dismissed the question with a wave of her hand. "Oh, nothing. Well, you two always have your heads together when it comes to me, and she's been dropping hints constantly."

The door opened. "Can we come in yet?"

"Uh oh. Maybe I did mention it to her," Jason hurriedly mumbled.

Leona walked in with a huge wicker basket. "Here's your dinner—lobster, corn on the cob, and sautéed new potatoes with parsley." She looked at Jason. "Did I forget anything?"

His head made a slight nod.

"Oh yeah, Danny, get the other basket in the trunk of my car."

After Danny left, Leona asked Jason, "What did she say?"

"I'm standing right here, Leona." Annie held up her left hand to show off the sparkling diamond ring on her finger.

Leona grabbed Annie's hand. "Camilla did a beautiful job crafting your ring. It's elegant but modest." Leona squealed with delight, picked up Annie and twirled her around. "So there is a chance I'll be a grandmother someday."

"If you don't get out of here, you might not live to see that day, though," Annie said as she pushed Leona to the door just as Danny was coming back in with another basket. "I'll take that, thank you very much." Annie took the basket before she pushed them both outside, slammed the door and locked it.

Jason roared with laughter. "I like it much better when someone else is the recipient of your stubborn behavior."

Annie already had the basket open and looked inside. "Oh, Leona made her fancy pumpkin cheesecake for dessert. How did she know that's my favorite?" Annie raised her eyebrows and looked at Jason.

"Come on, I was friends with Leona before I ever knew you existed. She's as close as a sister could be for me."

Her eyebrows inched higher.

Jason sighed. "We'll stop conspiring behind your back. But, for the record, it's always in your best interest."

Annie laughed. "I know, just giving you a hard time. You couldn't push Leona away even if you actually wanted to. It's kind of fun knowing that the two of you are always trying to make my life as good as it can be." She set the basket on the counter and wrapped her arms around Jason's neck.

"That's better," he mumbled into her curls. "Shall we eat or skip right to dessert?"

"We have all night. Let's take care of those lobsters. It would be a shame for them to go to waste."

One more kiss before they separated and then Jason refilled their champagne glasses and Annie brought the food to the table.

With soft music playing in the background, Annie let herself completely relax, enjoy the food and Jason's company. She finally shut out any thoughts of Christy and Eddie—until her phone beeped— but Jason shut it off and wouldn't let Annie check her messages.

She didn't complain.

***

Warm pumpkin scones, leftover pumpkin cheesecake, cut up melon and a pot of strong French roast coffee covered the table, where only the night before Annie enjoyed a delicious lobster dinner.

"I could get used to this treatment, Mr. Hunter," Annie said as she poured herself a cup of coffee. "I never even heard you get up. I must have slept like the dead."

"Not the dead since you were snoring like a chainsaw. I had to get up to get some peace and quiet."

Annie felt her cheeks begin to burn with embarrassment until she noticed Jason laughing. "You slept like a baby."

Jason started to toss Annie's phone on the table. "You can have this back, find out what was so darn urgent last night, but only if you promise to share every detail with me." He held the phone above Annie's head. "Promise?"

"Well, what if it's a message from my secret admirer?" she teased.

"In that case, I'm smashing your phone now." He put the phone on the floor and lifted his foot.

Annie tackled him, pushing him off balance and they both landed in a heap on the couch.

Annie tried to get up but Jason held her. The more she struggled, the tighter his arms closed around her until she was laughing so hard she gave up the struggle and relaxed on his chest. "You drive a hard bargain, but I promise to share everything about Christy and the murder with you."

"That was a win-win for me." He nuzzled her neck before relaxing his hold on her, but Annie didn't hop up. She settled in, resting her head beneath his chin.

A knock on the door got her moving.

"Geez, what now?" Jason said. "I might have to move you out of Catfish Cove if I ever hope to get time alone with you."

Annie stood up and straightened her disheveled clothes with one hand and raked her fingers through her wet hair with the other. Jason opened the door.

Tyler stood outside, looking a bit sheepish. "I tried Annie's apartment and there was no answer. She didn't answer her phone last night, so I stopped here to check if you knew where she was."

Jason moved out of the way so Tyler could see beyond him. Annie sat at the table drinking coffee and munching on a scone.

"Care to join us for breakfast?" Annie indicated a chair for Tyler.

"Oh, sorry, didn't mean to intrude." He started to turn around to leave.

Jason took his arm. "No problem. There's plenty of food. Come on in. You must have something important if you drove over here." Jason brought another mug and plate to the table for Tyler.

Tyler sat down. Annie poured him some coffee. His mouth dropped open when he took the mug from her hand. "What's this?" He touched her diamond ring.

Annie smiled shyly. "Last night. That's why my phone was off."

Tyler hugged Annie. "Congratulations." A tear slid down his cheek. After he straightened, he shook Jason's hand and slapped him on the back. "Good luck. She's got a mind of her own."

Jason nodded and smiled. "That she does."

Annie added a pumpkin scone to Tyler's plate. "What's so important? Did you discover something interesting about the mystery man, Dusty Reed?"

He nodded, his mouth too full to talk.

Jason gave Annie a quizzical look and mouthed the words, mystery man?

Tyler washed down the scone with a slug of coffee and wiped his mouth. "Yes, and you'll never guess in a million years what he's doing here in town."

Annie stood up. "Don't leave us hanging like that, Tyler Johnson. Is he here to kill Christy?"

Tyler held his hands up. "Nothing like that. I followed Dusty and Christy to her house last night to find out what was going on. They're working together."

Chapter 16

"He helped Christy kill Eddie?"

"Annie." Tyler gently put his hand over her mouth. "Let me finish before your mind makes up the completely wrong story. Dusty is an undercover cop. He signed up for the same class at Mixed Drinks Bartender School with Eddie, Samantha, Kyle and Dennis. He contacted Christy after he suspected Eddie was involved in a scam."

"Why didn't he arrest Eddie? According to what Samantha told me, Eddie had the money. Wasn't that enough evidence?"

"Christy thought she could handle it all herself. You know her, Annie, she's independent and more stubborn than you are. She thought if she had the money, she could lure Eddie away from his buddies, get her dog back, and arrest Eddie, or at least con him into revealing the whole scheme."

Jason, who was quietly finishing his coffee, put his cup down. "You women don't know when to ask for help, do you?"

Annie's eyes flashed. "Hey! I didn't lure anyone to town."

Jason winked at her and smiled. "Just kidding, but you are a tad defensive."

Tyler shook his head at the two lovebirds and continued, "Dusty was after the big fish in the scheme. The money was important, but when Christy left with the money, the others cooled it with the scam and Dusty had nothing to make an arrest."

"How did Dusty end up here at the same time as Eddie?"

"Dusty was keeping tabs on Eddie. He followed him on a hunch." Tyler sat back in his chair.

"So where does that leave us?" Annie asked.

"There's no *us* in this Annie. Christy didn't kill Eddie. I have three suspects and they're each dangerous and could kill again. They want the money. They want to get their scam up and running again. The only good thing about all this is that Samantha, Kyle and Dennis don't trust each other. They'll point the finger at anyone, and if they find the money, there will be less people to split it between. And, this is important, they don't know about Dusty being an undercover cop. As long as he's part of their group, he has a certain amount of influence and can keep a step ahead of events."

Annie stood up to clear the table, mumbling, "That did a lot of good to keep Eddie alive."

Tyler reached out and snatched another pumpkin scone, ignoring Annie's comment. "These are delicious. Did you make them?" he asked Annie.

"Leona surprised us with two baskets of food last night. A lobster dinner, pumpkin cheesecake for dessert, and these scones for breakfast."

"Pumpkin cheesecake? Is there any left?"

"Sure." She cut Tyler a generous piece and slid it onto his plate. "You want this second scone too?"

He puckered his lips in thought. "No, the cheesecake will hit the spot."

Annie carried everything except Tyler's plate to the kitchen. "I'm curious."

Jason rolled his eyes and laughed. "Of course you are."

She ignored his comment. "What's the scam?"

Tyler savored his first bite of cheesecake. "Oh, delicious. So creamy and just the right amount of sweetness and spices."

Annie stomped her foot. "Tyler Johnson, I'll take that cheesecake away if you don't stop treating me like I'm an imbecile. I know exactly what you're doing and I don't like to be ignored."

Tyler laughed. "The scam? I don't know all the details, but they made random phone calls and convinced whoever answered that their grandson or granddaughter was in trouble and needed money as soon as possible. Quite clever if you ask me. Of course, once Grandma found out her grandson or granddaughter was home safe and sound and not in a bit of trouble, there would be no traceable phone number and the money was gone."

"Christy stole the money from Eddie before she knew Dusty was investigating?"

"Uh huh. If he got Eddie with the money, he thinks he could have gotten more names. No money, and now, no Eddie."

"Christy has the money. Maybe that was her goal. Keep the money and get rid of all the other players," Annie said quietly.

Tyler stood up. "Aww, come on Annie. Christy's not a criminal."

"How can you be so sure? She's your girlfriend. How can you be impartial? Maybe it's her variation of vigilante justice."

Tyler brought his plate to the sink. "Watch yourself. I'm not listening to any more of your crazy talk." He stomped out the door.

After the echo of the slamming door quieted, Jason started to load the dishwasher. "You hit a nerve. His reaction makes me think that somewhere in his head, he agrees with you."

"Tyler calls me stubborn, but he needs to look in the mirror. I've known him my whole life and his stubbornness can blind him to what's about to smack him in the face."

"I don't think I like the direction this is heading. You're going to keep snooping around since you don't trust Tyler to do his job properly."

With her hands on her hips, Annie scowled at Jason. "Don't you care if the right person that murdered Eddie is found?"

"Of course I do, but how can you be so sure Tyler isn't finding that person?"

"What if Samantha is right and Christy manipulates the evidence to target someone else?"

"What if Samantha's manipulating you, Annie? She's involved in an illegal scam worth a lot of money. I would say that makes her untrustworthy. What has Tyler or Christy done to make you think you can't trust them?"

Annie and Jason stared at each other. Jason was first to look away and sigh. "I know nothing will stop you, short of me locking you in a room and force feeding you champagne and cheesecake." He grinned, then got serious again. "Be careful, this could get ugly, especially if you're right about Christy."

A loud knocking interrupted them and Roxy ran to the door, barking. Someone was turning the knob but it was still locked.

"I'll bet you the last piece of cheesecake I know who that is," Jason said as he walked to the door. "Well?" He waited for an answer from Annie without opening the door.

"No deal. We can split the cheesecake. Of course it's Leona with some lame excuse why she had to show up bright and early."

As soon as Jason began to pull the door open, it burst inward with a force knocking him off balance.

"I hope you don't mind. We waited as long as possible," Leona said as she bounced in followed by Danny, Mia, Martha and Camilla.

"Who's at the café?" Annie asked.

"We all met there but I decided we can open a little late today. It's not busy until mid-morning on a Sunday anyway." She set her bag on the counter and started unpacking all sorts of goodies.

Congratulations were said all around and Camilla had to inspect the ring. "Are you happy with it? Jason told me exactly how he wanted it designed, you know. *Exactly*."

"So you all knew about this before I did?" Annie said, throwing her arms in the air.

Silence—for five seconds—before everyone started talking at once. "Jason needed help," Leona explained, handing a glass to Annie. She passed glasses around the room. "A toast to Annie and Jason."

"What are we drinking?" Annie asked as she took a sip. "Delicious."

"Mimosas, but straight OJ for Danny." Next, Leona carried a tray around filled with slices of pumpkin roll, pumpkin chocolate chip muffins, and thin slices of pumpkin cheesecake.

Annie groaned with her hands over her stomach. "I can't eat another thing."

She topped off Annie's glass and whispered in her ear, "You look shell-shocked."

"A little more time alone would have been nice."

"Tyler was already here so we figured it was our turn."

"How do you know Tyler was here?"

"He stopped at the café looking for you. He said you never answered your phone last night and he was concerned. Don't worry, I didn't spoil the surprise of your engagement. What did he say?"

"He told Jason good luck, I've got a mind of my own, or something along those lines."

Leona laughed a deep belly laugh. "And don't change." She gave Annie a bone crushing hug before moving on to refill everyone else's glass and stopping to chat with Jason.

Annie smiled. She couldn't complain about her family and friends even if they didn't give her an ounce of privacy at times. She wouldn't trade them for anything.

Camilla's voice was soft and soothing at her side. "It was so hard to keep the ring a secret from you. You know, with my habit of letting everything flop out of my mouth."

Annie held her hand up and admired the ring. "It's beautiful and extra special to me knowing you made it."

"Jason was so worried you would hear us talking about it, or get upset that I was over here so often lately. You're lucky. I can't imagine finding someone as wonderful as Jason." She sighed, momentarily lost in her thoughts. "What do you think about Dusty?"

"Besides the fact that he left you stranded last night? That doesn't put him high on my list of good date qualities."

"There is that," her eyes widened, "but isn't he about the most handsome guy in Catfish Cove?"

"Yes, he's easy on the eyes, but what else do you know about him? Did he ever tell you why he's really here in town?"

Camilla's eyes narrowed. "Don't tell me he's a murderer. My radar can't be that bad."

"No, I don't think it's that bad, but he is involved, one way or another." Annie bit her tongue before giving too much information to Camilla about Dusty. It wouldn't do anyone any good if his undercover work became common knowledge.

Camilla whispered in Annie's ear, "He did tell me he's been keeping an eye on Christy. He thinks she might be involved in some sort of scam."

Annie's eyes darted to Camilla's before searching the room for Jason. Their eyes met, his expression questioning Annie about what was going on with Camilla.

Chapter 17

Annie flopped onto Jason's comfy couch the second the door closed behind Leona, the last one to leave. "The day has only started and I'm already exhausted from the intrusions."

Jason put the last of the dirty dishes in the dishwasher and pressed start. "So, a nice lazy day? Just you and me?"

Roxy whined. "And Roxy," Jason said as he filled a bowl with her food. "We could take a walk along the Lake Trail."

Annie didn't budge.

"Or not." Jason sat next to Annie.

"That's actually a good idea," she said. "Fresh air and some exercise will wake me up. Let's go."

Jason handed Annie her fleece and he pulled on a warm sweatshirt. Roxy waited by the door, dancing with impatience.

"I should check on Smokey first. He's independent, especially with his cat door, but I should make sure he's okay."

Annie made a quick detour into her apartment to find everything quiet and Smokey content on the couch. She filled his water and food bowls before hurrying back outside with Jason and Roxy.

They walked arm in arm along the Lake Trail. No talking, just the crunch of their feet on the path.

Annie noticed Thelma Dodd sitting in her rocker on her porch that overlooked the lake. She waved.

"Let's visit Thelma. I don't visit often enough and she'll be thrilled to hear the news about our engagement."

"Doesn't she always want help with her crossword puzzle?" Jason reminded Annie.

"Maybe you can distract her with your charm."

Thelma was already at the door by the time they followed the narrow path that led to her kitchen entryway. "Come in. Come in. It's wonderful to have some company on this beautiful morning. And you have your dog, too. Let me get some biscuits for her."

Thelma's cane thumped on the linoleum and her cupboard door squeaked open. Roxy's ears perked up at the sound of the dog bones. She sat patiently, watching Thelma return.

"Here you go." Roxy, very gently, took the dog bone from Thelma's fingers. "What a sweet girl." She turned her attention to Annie and Jason. "Do you have time for some hot tea?"

"That would be perfect," Annie said.

"The kettle's still hot. Help yourself and come join me on the porch." Thelma slowly made her way back to her chair and settled down next to her table and newspaper.

Annie and Jason followed with their tea.

"Now, what news do you have for me?" Thelma asked, looking at Annie and resting her hand on Roxy's head.

"Well," Annie smiled, "I do have a bit of news." She looked at Jason. "We're engaged as of last night." Her face broke into a grin from ear to ear.

Thelma clapped her hands together. "Wonderful. Just wonderful. It's about time young man." She looked at Jason over the top of her glasses. "You didn't want to let this young lady get away, now did you?"

"No, I wasn't going to let that happen." Jason reached for Annie's hand.

Annie looked at the view from Thelma's porch. "Have you been seeing lots of people on the Lake Trail?"

"Not too many. I always see you and your dog and I see that new detective in town. She walks the trail all the time."

Annie's ears perked up. "Detective Christy Crank? Do you know her?"

Thelma pulled her white cardigan sweater tighter around her shoulders and fumbled with the buttons, closing them right up to her chin. "I only know her from her picture in the Catfish Cove Chronicle when she got hired. She's a cute little thing. Maybe I'm old fashioned, but I don't understand how she could be a detective. The world has changed since I was young, that's for sure."

Annie sipped her tea, cradling the mug in her hands for extra warmth. "When did you last see her?"

"Not for the last couple of nights. I think it was the night before Halloween. Yes, that's it. She was in a big hurry and she kept looking over her shoulder. There was someone else behind her but he was quite far back."

"He?"

"Oh, I'm not sure. It could have been a she, I guess. I don't think they were together." Thelma picked up her paper. "Now, maybe you two could help me with a couple of these clues for my crossword puzzle." She looked at Jason and Annie over her reading glasses. "Are you ready?"

They nodded.

"Okay, this one has me stumped even though I feel like the answer is right at the tip of my tongue. A six letter word ending with N that is deadly." She pursed her lips. "My brain is stuck on venom or toxin but those are only five letters."

Annie hesitantly said, "Poison?"

"Of course!" Thelma erased something she had already written and scribbled the new word on the puzzle. "I always work with a pencil so I can fix my mistakes."

Jason leaned back and crossed his legs. "What other clues do you have? This sounds like an interesting puzzle."

"It's the Halloween puzzle. I'm a little behind," she added. "Let's see, how about an eight letter word that means murder?"

Annie was starting to feel uneasy with the talk about poison and murder but Jason enjoyed the mind challenge.

"Any letters yet?" Jason asked.

Thelma shook her head.

Jason counted on his fingers. "Massacre would fit."

Annie blurted out, "Homicide," at the same moment.

"Yes!" Thelma exclaimed. "You're good at this Annie. I'll write homicide in for now and see if it fits with the rest of the words." She filled in the squares and read the next clue. "Well, this one is easy, a red body fluid has to be blood and it fits with the 'o' in homicide. I wonder who thinks up this stuff. This puzzle is kind of gory." She set her newspaper on the table. "I'll work more on it later, I want to sit and watch the world go by for a while."

Annie stood. "Thanks for the tea, Thelma. Don't get up, we'll let ourselves out."

"Stop in anytime, you two. And congratulations. Young love." Her eyes glazed over and Annie imagined Thelma's mind drifting to some pleasant memory from her past.

Annie carried the empty cups to the sink and rinsed them. Jason opened the door for Annie and Roxy, pulling it closed behind them with barely a sound to disturb Thelma.

"Interesting crossword puzzle. Your brain jumped to the right words immediately," Jason commented to Annie before he wrapped his arm around her shoulder as they headed down the path to the Lake Trail.

"Well, yeah, poison, homicide, blood— that's pretty much what happened right here on Halloween eve. I'm glad she didn't keep going; my skin was starting to crawl."

Their strides matched perfectly as they settled into a fast pace. Roxy sniffed and darted every which way, exploring off the trail.

"Okay, I'll bite. What are you thinking?" Jason asked.

"I'm still wondering if Eddie's body was checked for poison. It would have been easy for someone working at the Catfish Cove Pub to slip something in his drink. He spent a lot of time hanging out at the bar, apparently annoying everyone there. Lots of details about Eddie and Christy don't match up depending on whose version of the story you hear, but there was at least one thing everyone did have in common." She stopped walking. "No one was particularly fond of Eddie."

Jason nodded in agreement. "I can't argue with that statement, but if he was poisoned, how did he get to the Cove's Corner parking lot to meet Christy?"

"I did some research. There are slow acting poisons." Annie watched her feet as she walked.

"But how could the murderer time the poison so Eddie could get to his meeting with Christy?"

She stopped and turned toward Jason, shrugging her shoulders. "I don't know. Maybe that was just a convenient plus for the murderer."

Annie called Roxy and turned around, heading back to Jason's house.

"It's an interesting theory, for sure. What do you plan to do next?"

"Make a visit to Tyler."

Chapter 18

Jason checked the time. "I can't go with you, is that okay?"

"To be honest, I like it better. No offense, but Tyler will be more open with me if I'm alone. And, you know," she held up her left hand so the sun glinted off her ring, "there's no need for that tiny jealous streak of yours to pop up anymore."

Jason's mouth fell open. "Jealous?"

Annie bumped her shoulder into Jason's side. "Yes, jealous."

He wrapped his arms around her and mumbled into her sweet smelling hair. "You're right. I couldn't help it whenever I saw the two of you talking together."

"He'll always be one of my best friends. You're okay with that, aren't you?" Annie looked into Jason's eyes.

"Yes, and Leona is my best friend. After you," he quickly added.

"Fair enough." Annie kept her arm looped through Jason's as they turned up the path to his house.

Annie sighed gratefully as she drove past the Black Cat Café. She was thankful that Leona didn't need her help at the café since Mia and Martha both insisted they could cover for Annie to give her a day off. Of course, they expected her to be spending the time with Jason, but what they didn't know wouldn't upset them.

The police station was quiet when Annie entered. She nodded to the woman on duty and explained that she needed to talk to the police chief as soon as possible.

"Go ahead down the hall, last door on the left."

Annie was puzzling to herself how she would bring up the subject of poison without Tyler laughing her right out of his office when she overheard him say the word poison. Who was he talking to? His office door was ajar so she poked her head around the corner before knocking and disturbing him.

Tyler sat hunched over his desk, completely engrossed on the telephone, nodding but saying nothing. He scribbled in the pad open in front of him before saying a quick thanks and hanging up. His chair creaked as his weight shifted backward and he leaned into his hands laced behind his head.

Annie pushed the door enough to squeeze inside. "Busy?" she asked.

Tyler's eyes focused on Annie, and the faraway look in his eyes cleared when he registered her presence. "Yes, but come on in."

She made herself comfortable in the only unoccupied chair. Two other chairs were pushed up against the wall holding stacks of manila folders.

"It's always like that on the weekend. All those files will be put away tomorrow. I can never keep up with the paperwork." He leaned forward with both elbows on his desk and his chin resting on his overlapping fingers. "What can I do for you, Annie?"

She decided there was no beating around the bush with her latest thought about Eddie's murder. "Is there any chance Eddie was poisoned?"

Tyler's hands dropped onto his desk, his eyes narrowed and his face leaned as close as possible toward Annie. "Poison? Why would you ask that?"

She held her hands up, palms toward Tyler. "Just a crazy thought I had when I was sitting at the pub the other night, and then again today something came up in a crossword puzzle. I had to ask."

Tyler grinned and leaned back in his chair. "So, you didn't find a vial of poison on the beach or anything like that?"

"No, nothing that obvious. Did you?"

"No, that would make my job way to easy. I like a challenge. Let's start with the pub. What happened there?"

"They were serving a drink called Poison Punch."

He raised his eyebrows.

Annie continued. "It got me thinking how easy it would have been for someone working behind the bar to serve an actual poisoned drink to a customer. Especially someone like Eddie who hung out at the bar annoying everyone."

"Annoying people isn't exactly a reason to murder them. The owner could ask him to leave, or call us and say he was disturbing the peace. And the crossword puzzle? I can't wait to hear how that ties in."

Annie stood up. "Never mind. If you aren't going to take me seriously, I'm not going to sit here so you can make fun of me."

Tyler stood up, reaching the door before Annie could. He shut it and gently pushed her back to the chair. "Sorry. I'm all ears and," he made an X across his chest, "no laughing. Promise."

She sat back down and Tyler returned to his chair. "I was helping Thelma Dodd with her crossword puzzle and the answers were poison and homicide. I know all this sounds crazy and it's only a theory but why not check it out?"

Tyler pursed his lips. "Just before you walked in, I got a call from the coroner's lab. He found traces of arsenic in Eddie's body."

Annie's eyes widened in surprise. "Is that what killed him? Not Christy stabbing him or the wound on his head?"

"Probably not. But it does indicate someone had the intention of slowly poisoning him."

"Why?"

"A bigger cut of the scam money would be my guess."

"Maybe Eddie double crossed someone in the group and he came to Catfish Cove to beg Christy for help."

"I don't do 'maybes.' I shouldn't even be hazarding a guess. But if you came up with the poison theory, someone else might too. Don't blab it around town and put yourself in danger, Annie."

She stood up to leave. "One more thing. What about Eddie's computer? Does Christy know that *you* know it's still in her house?"

He shook his head. "I'm still trying to figure that one out. What's your theory?"

"Honestly?" She twisted her mouth into a grimace and shook her head. "I've got nothing."

They both laughed.

"I think that's the first time you have ever come up empty of a theory or a feeling."

Annie walked to her car. She might not have a theory or a feeling about Christy's plan with Eddie's computer, but she could certainly try to find one."

She made a quick stop at the café to pick up a bribe and formulate a plan.

"Hey, where's your fiancé?" Leona shouted when Annie walked into the café. "You came for more treats to boost your energy levels?"

Annie didn't mind Leona, Mia and Martha getting a chuckle at her expense. She could go with Leona's suggestion to avoid telling them her real mission.

Leona already had a box open, filling it with a variety of pumpkin treats—muffins, scones, bread and two single-serve cheesecakes.

"Don't eat this all in one sitting or you won't fit in your wedding dress," Leona teased.

Annie's eyes narrowed into small dark slits. "What wedding dress?"

Leona doubled over laughing. "Any wedding dress. Don't worry; I didn't pick one out for you yet. I thought that would be a good project for tomorrow."

Annie picked up the box of goodies and dismissed all their laughter with a wave of her hand as she left the café.

"Christy Crank, here I come," Annie said to herself. "If this doesn't sweeten you up and loosen your tongue, nothing will."

Two cars were parked in Christy's driveway. "Well, well, well, my lucky day."

She picked up her box, glad there was plenty for three, and headed to Christy's front door.

Bella's and Blue's barking and jumping on the door made the house shake before Christy pushed them aside and got the door opened.

"Oh, this is a surprise." Christy looked around Annie as she pulled her inside. "Did you come alone?"

"Just me and some delicious pumpkin treats from the Black Cat Café," Annie said, holding up the box.

Christy turned her head, looking toward her kitchen but didn't invite Annie any further into her house. "What are you doing here?"

"Bringing something to go with your coffee. You do have coffee, don't you?"

Dusty poked his head through the kitchen door. "I'll get the coffee going. Where are your manners, Christy?"

Christy whispered, "You shouldn't be here. Drink your coffee and leave."

Annie walked into the kitchen. She almost dropped the box when she saw Eddie's computer sitting on Christy's counter. She pretended to trip to cover herself but she didn't miss Christy's eyes dart to the laptop. No time to be bashful, she told herself.

"How did you manage to get Eddie's computer back?"

"The details aren't important, just the information we're finding on it," Christy quickly replied.

Dusty turned around. "Yeah, we found some great information."

Annie tried to keep her face neutral, afraid to reveal her worries. Christy turned her back to Annie and pulled a cookie tray out of the oven.

The smell of something roasted filled the kitchen. "What are you cooking?"

Dusty sat behind the computer. "We found Eddie's roasted pumpkin seed recipe. He was a real addict and kept trying different spices along with the butter and salt. This is his latest."

Christy slid the hot seeds onto a plate. "Try one. Tell me what you think."

Annie hesitantly picked up one pumpkin seed, not sure if this was some type of trap. She juggled the seed between her two hands and blew on it. Looking up at the other two she asked, "Aren't you going to try one?"

Christy laughed. "Don't worry, Annie. They aren't *poisoned* or anything."

Annie's legs felt weak so she let herself slide into a chair at the kitchen table.

"Poison? Why would you say something like that?"

Chapter 19

Christy sat across from Annie. "You're as white as a sheet. What's going on?"

"Someone tried to poison Eddie. Didn't you know?"

Dusty swiveled his chair around to face the two women sitting at the table. Christy's mouth opened and closed a couple of times before any words came out. "He said something about me trying to poison him just as he lunged toward me. I thought it was crazy talk at the time. Did Tyler tell you this?"

Annie nodded. "Reluctantly. Only after I told him my theory."

A smile crept onto Christy's face. "Of course, your theories." She held her hand up quickly. "I don't mean that as an insult."

Dusty remained silent. Stone faced. Annie's eyes darted between Christy and Dusty.

Christy popped a handful of the cooled pumpkin seeds into her mouth. "See? No poison. The secret ingredient is cayenne pepper. You don't notice it with the first crunch, but the heat builds gradually. We've been experimenting on the amount to add." She waved her hand in front of her mouth. "Here comes the heat." She looked at Dusty. "I think we got this batch just right."

Dusty finally said something. "You must be wondering how I fit into all this. Especially after I so inelegantly deserted your friend last night."

Annie opened the box of treats she brought from the café with shaky fingers. Her mind raced with dreadful images. All with her ending in a bloody mangled heap on an abandoned dead end dirt road. What did she walk into?

Christy reached across the table, gently placing her hand on Annie's arm. "Dusty," she nodded her head in his direction, "and I are working on this together. We have found important information on Eddie's computer. Besides the pumpkin seed recipe." She smiled, trying to lighten the mood.

"The computer? No one actually stole it?"

"Listen." Christy softened her voice. "I had to make it look real. Make everyone believe it was stolen to take the pressure off me for a few days. Dusty was the person you saw in my house. It was all planned to make whoever was watching my house think someone involved in the scam stole it. With Eddie dead, they're all suspecting each other and someone will make a mistake. It's a matter of time."

Annie stood up and paced in Christy's kitchen. "Matter of time? Before what? Someone else gets killed?"

Christy sighed. "I tried to tell you to stay out of this. Yes, it's dangerous, but our goal is to find Eddie's killer and the snake head of this scam. If we don't find that person, he'll just move it somewhere else and more people will be in danger."

"He? You know it's a he?"

Dusty looked in Annie's box of baked treats. "All things pumpkin in here?" He didn't wait for an answer before he chose a chocolate chip pumpkin muffin. "Is the coffee ready yet?"

Christy took three mugs from her cupboard. "All you think about is your stomach." She poured coffee and put a jug of milk and a box of sugar on her counter. "Help yourselves."

"And what about Camilla? That was a really underhanded move you pulled on her last night." Annie stared at Dusty as he poured his coffee, his back muscles tense.

Christy flicked her wrist. "Camilla will get over it. We had to make sure she didn't get in the way of our investigation."

Dusty turned around. "I like Camilla. I should never have let myself get into that situation while I'm working on a case. Maybe when this is over . . ." His words trailed off and Annie saw the pain in his face.

"Camilla is too forgiving. But *I'm* not. You owe her an apology at the very least," Annie told Dusty.

Christy slammed her hand on the table. "What aren't you getting about this conversation, Annie? One person has already been killed. If you care about Camilla, you'll keep her away from Dusty like I told you last night." Her eyes glared into Annie's. "And you'll make yourself scarce, too. What is it with you, always thinking you know better than the rest of us?"

Annie stood up. Fury filled her body; fury at Christy for treating her like an imbecile; fury at herself for thinking she could talk sense into a control freak like Christy.

Christy's voice mellowed and she grabbed Annie's hand. "What's that on your finger?"

Annie twisted her ring, not used to the feel yet. Light from the kitchen made it sparkle and she smiled, despite her anger.

Christy embraced her. "You lucky stubborn woman." Christy kept her hands on Annie's shoulders and stood at an arm's distance. "Jason finally got up enough courage to pop the question?"

Afraid to talk and betray her emotions, Annie nodded in response to Christy's question.

Dusty, back at Eddie's computer, blurted out, "I found something interesting."

Christy rushed to his side. Annie looked over her shoulder.

"Did you ever look in his spam folder?"

"I don't remember, probably not. What did you find?" Christy pushed her glasses higher on her nose.

Dusty clicked on a folder labeled *Recipes*. A list of documents opened, all including the word *recipe*. "He must have planned to empty this but never did before he was killed."

Christy pointed to a document labeled *Recipe for Revenge*. "Open that one."

Annie shivered as she skimmed down the 'recipe' which included exactly how Eddie planned to move to Catfish Cove, manipulate Christy by using her dog Blue, get the money back, and con the others in the group.

"Was he the mastermind?" Christy asked Dusty.

"I don't know. I always wondered why he was the one to have the money. It was a little risky to hide it right under the nose of a police officer."

"Smart, if you ask me," Annie said. "The perfect cover. Who would find it there except you, Christy?"

Dusty turned around. "How *did* you find the money, Christy? Were you involved? Did you double-cross your husband at the time?"

Annie watched Christy closely. Her behavior had been odd for the past few days, leaving Annie with questions about Christy's story and whereabouts. "Were you on the Lake Trail Halloween Eve? With someone following you?"

Christy backed up. Her face drained of color. Her mouth hung open and her eyes grew big and round. "What are you two saying?" she hissed before focusing on Annie. "I was on the Lake Trail, rushing to your house, pretending to be stabbed. Remember? My costume preview?"

Possible, Annie thought. She didn't know the exact time Thelma Dodd saw Christy.

Christy turned her attention to Dusty. "I can't believe you don't trust me. I've shared everything I know with you. For your information, I took the money in a moment of rage and fear. I didn't know where the money came from, but when I found it I knew where it was going. With me. That slimy creep. I had to get away from him." Her shoulders sagged as she leaned on the wall for support. "I felt like my whole life had been ripped out from under me and all I could do was run away. Run for my life."

Annie's heart went out to Christy. She completely identified with her fear and reaction. Annie had done the same only a little over a year ago. "But why Catfish Cove?" Annie had fled to Catfish Cove, back to her family.

"Why not?" I holed up in a motel for a week, making a plan, searching for a job. Christy shrugged. "I had to make a decision, and here I am. Dusty, if you don't believe that I'm in this for the right reasons, leave. Walk out that door right now. It's about time you left anyway before someone gets suspicious of your car being in my driveway for so long."

Dusty turned his attention back to the computer. "Sorry. I had to clear that up for myself. You can't blame me. Everyone's a potential suspect lately." He slid off the stool. "Keep searching this file and let me know if you find anything else. I'll let myself out."

The door slammed closed, leaving Annie wondering what was next. "Where's the money?"

Christy sat in front of the computer, pulling her ponytail tighter. "Huh? What money?"

"The money you stole from Eddie." Annie sat at the table facing Christy, sipping on her lukewarm coffee.

"I buried it," she replied, glancing quickly out the kitchen window.

Annie laughed out loud. "Brilliant. Let me guess, it's in your raised bed under the pumpkin vine."

"Annie, you amaze me at times. Who would think of that but you?" She laughed, too, but didn't confirm or deny the guess.

"Don't worry, I don't plan on poking around out there. Your secret is safe with me. What do we do next?" Annie finished her coffee and carried the mug to the sink. She rinsed hers and Dusty's, setting them on the drying mat next to the sink.

"You are one crazy, stubborn friend. Next? We figure out who killed Eddie." Christy leaned back and closed the laptop with a snap.

Annie's lips curled into a grin. Christy called her a friend *and* she used the word we. "Great. I have an idea."

"Of course you do. I would expect nothing less from you. Let's hear it."

Chapter 20

"First, we're going to the Black Cat Café for some lunch. I have today off so I'm looking forward to being served instead of doing the serving." Annie smiled.

Christy slid her computer into a high kitchen cupboard. "Just in case. I know Tyler has a backup of the information but I don't want to have to ask him for it."

Annie's head whipped around. "You know about that?"

Christy chuckled. "You need to keep your emotions hidden better. I didn't actually know, but I suspected. Of course he would keep the information safe. I would have done the same thing. Now, let's go. Suddenly, I'm ravenous."

The brunch crowd was in full swing when they arrived at the café. "I don't believe this," Annie whispered. "We'll have to wait for a seat."

"I don't mind, lets me people watch and enjoy being out of my house." She elbowed Annie. "Look who's all cozy with their heads together over in the corner booth?"

"I should be working." With that, Annie grabbed an apron and a pot of coffee and sauntered over to the booth with Dennis, Kyle, and Samantha.

"Enjoying brunch?" Annie asked, putting on her friendliest smile. "More coffee?"

Samantha smiled at Annie and held out her cup. "Thanks." Kyle sat stone-faced, ignoring Annie. Dennis held out his cup but remained quiet.

"What's up with her?" Samantha tilted her head, indicating where Christy was standing.

Annie slid in next to Samantha. "That's exactly what I'm trying to figure out. I heard she's a suspect in Eddie's death. Do you think she did it?"

Annie saw Kyle's head turn slightly in her direction and Samantha leaned toward Annie. "I always suspected her. Poor Eddie. He only came here to Catfish Cove to get what was rightfully his. She'll probably laugh all the way to the bank and someone else will get blamed for his murder."

Dennis glared at Samantha. "What are you blabbering about? Eddie was an annoying moron. He got what he deserved."

Kyle's eyes moved between Samantha and Dennis, then settled on Annie's face. "We didn't invite you to sit with us. What were you doing at the detective's house this morning?" He threw a handful of pumpkin seeds into his mouth, chewing with his mouth open, looking at Annie with narrowed eyes.

"Dropping off an order from the bakery." Annie leaned in closer, hoping they didn't notice the shaking of her hands. She shook off his rudeness, determined to make the situation work for her. "Guess who was at her house?"

Samantha took the bait and asked, "Who?"

"Dusty Reed. Did he know Eddie?" Annie asked them in a hushed voice, keeping one eye on Christy the whole time.

Samantha shrugged. "Dusty knew Eddie at bartender school. Maybe Eddie introduced Dusty and Christy. I don't know."

"So what's she doing here?" Kyle asked and bits of seeds spewed from his mouth.

Annie returned Kyle's stare. "Good question. You'd better keep an eye on her." With that comment, she stood up, refilled Kyle's cup even though he didn't ask for more coffee, and walked behind the counter.

Leona gave her a quizzical look. "What are you doing? Did you forget this is your day off?"

"Nope," she said as she walked by Leona. "Just trying to get some information from those three clowns. One of them has to be the murderer." She packed up a piece of broccoli quiche, some spinach salad, and a fruit smoothie. She raised her arm and motioned for Christy to come to the cash register.

"What are you doing?" Christy hissed.

"Here's your order," Annie said and held her hand out for payment.

"What's in the bag?" Christy asked as she looked inside. "Aren't we going to sit and enjoy a leisurely lunch together?"

"Plans changed. I hope you like quiche and spinach salad. It's what was ready."

Christy smiled. "My favorite. Why are you drawing attention to me?"

"Giving them something to worry about, and I had to explain to Kyle why I was at your house. Apparently, he drove by and saw my car," she whispered to Christy. Handing Christy her change, Annie said, "Don't look now, but trouble may have just walked through the door."

Of course, Christy whipped her head around to see Tyler stride in. Instead of approaching Christy, he poured himself a cup of coffee. He took a sip, surveyed the room and then made his way to the booth with Dennis, Kyle, and Samantha.

Tyler spoke quietly to the three clowns. Kyle frowned, stood up and followed him out of the cafe. Samantha and Dennis slugged the rest of their coffee, threw money on the table, and hurried out too.

Christy turned back toward Annie. "I don't like not knowing what's going on. He must have found some evidence to bring Kyle in for questioning."

She started to follow Tyler but Annie grabbed her arm. "You can't follow them. They think you're a suspect."

With her eyes narrowed into slits, Christy clenched her teeth and asked Annie, "Why do they think I'm a suspect?"

"I told them you might be." She busied herself brushing invisible crumbs off the counter, avoiding Christy's glare.

Christy sighed. "I guess it could be worse."

"You're not mad at me?"

Christy laughed. "No. I'm only a make-believe suspect. I can live with that. Now, I'm going home to dig some holes in my backyard to see if I can find a buried treasure."

"You're what?"

"Just kidding," she whispered in Annie's ear. "The loots already hidden where no one will find it. I'm going to search for more hidden clues on Eddie's computer." She held up her bagged lunch. "Thanks. My mouth is already watering."

The café was beginning to clear out. Annie wrapped up some more quiche, made two more smoothies, hung up her apron, and headed to the door.

"Leaving so soon?" Leona shouted.

Annie held up her empty hand and waved. "I'll be back."

Camilla was alone in the gallery, sitting in the office reading a paperback romance while the pink nail polish dried on her outstretched hands.

"I brought you some lunch." Annie took out the two pieces of quiche, setting one in front of Camilla and giving her one of the smoothies. Annie sat in the other chair with her share of the food.

"I didn't expect to see you today; thanks for stopping by. It's kind of slow and boring so far. I was keeping my fingers crossed, hoping Dusty would come in. Ya know, I could yell at him for dumping me last night. At least, *that* might make me feel a bit better." She picked up the smoothie and took a long drink. "This is delicious. What's in it?"

"Strawberries, yogurt, maple syrup, and a banana—easy, filling, and yummy. Don't be too hard on yourself. I'm not sure yet, but Dusty might not be a *total* jerk. The jury's still out." Annie took a bite of her quiche.

"Really?" Camilla leaned forward. "Tell me more, Annie. He's way too cute to give up on if there's any chance he might be a legit catch."

"Well, I'm still looking into his background. Be patient."

Camilla put her book upside down on the desk and blew on her nails. "What do you know so far?" She sighed a deep, despairing sigh. "Give me some hope. This romance I'm reading is a poor substitute for a real hot guy I can touch with my pink fingernails." She wiggled her fingers and her eyebrows.

Annie burst out laughing. "You are *so* dramatic. I can't tell you anything else at the moment, but if you bump into him, go ahead and wink. He'll probably blush and stutter and make a complete fool of himself. You do that to guys, you know."

"I wish that were true; it's more like they always make a fool out of me."

Annie stood up. "Back to blond? The black hair didn't last too long."

Camilla shook her head, making her hair swirl around her face. "Every time I looked in the mirror I couldn't figure out who was looking back at me with black hair. It *so* wasn't me. Maybe Dusty likes blondes better?" she asked hopefully.

"Time will tell. Gotta run. You're okay here for the day?"

"Sure. I hope business picks up, though. I'm not crazy about having only myself for company all day."

"The café was mobbed. If you're lucky, some of those customers will wander in here and buy lots of artwork." Annie waved on her way out.

"Next stop, the police station," she mumbled to herself as she climbed into her car. "With any luck, Tyler will be done with Kyle and he'll have time to talk to me."

Annie's phone beeped with a text message before she had a chance to start her car. Digging her phone from her jeans pocket she saw a message from Christy, *something's not right.*

Annie headed her car to Christy's house to find out what was wrong instead of having a text conversation. Christy's car was in the driveway. Everything looked normal.

Except, as Annie pulled into the driveway, Blue and Bella charged from the back of the house to greet her car. Annie's senses jumped to high alert. Christy didn't usually let both of the dogs out together unless she was with them. Where was Christy?

Chapter 21

Annie opened her car door and greeted the two dogs. She had a couple of dog treats in her pocket so she patted the dogs, made them sit, and rewarded each with a cookie. She kept the corner of her eye on Christy's house, expecting to see her at any moment. The house was quiet. Too quiet.

Bella and Blue danced around Annie's legs once they were done cleaning up all the crumbs from their treat. "What should we do now?" Annie asked them. Tails wagged and dark brown eyes stared at her. They waited for Annie to make a decision for them all.

"Okay, then, let's go inside and see what we find." Talking out loud gave Annie added confidence as if there was someone with her besides the two canines. She walked toward the front door, glancing through the big front window for any movement.

Nothing. No birds singing, no cars driving by, just silence. The quiet felt eerie and unnatural.

The front door was unlocked, so Annie let herself and the dogs in the house. More silence. Blue dashed into the kitchen, followed by Bella, and finally Annie.

Annie gasped when she saw Christy sprawled on the floor. Blue licked her face. Christy moaned and tried to move away from the warm tongue. Her hand reached to her head as her eyes opened. "What happened?" she asked Annie.

Annie knelt beside her friend. "Good question. I just got here. Do you remember anything?"

Christy closed her eyes. "Something wasn't right, but I can't remember what. And now you're here."

"You sent me a text." Annie pulled Christy's phone from under her leg and found the last text she sent to Annie. Annie showed her the message.

Christy licked her lips and then bit the corner of her bottom lip. She pulled herself up onto one elbow. "I remember sending that, then nothing. Someone must have been in here. Waiting."

"Didn't the dogs bark?" Annie asked. She put her hands under Christy's armpits and helped her onto one of the kitchen chairs.

"I let them out and I was tying my shoes. Whoever was here must have whacked me over the head." She touched a spot on the back of her head. "Ouch." She looked at blood on her fingers and took Annie's hand, guiding it to her head. "Feel this."

Annie gently touched a huge bump. "I'll get you some ice." While she wrapped ice in a towel, she heard Christy talking to Tyler, telling him to come over.

Christy grimaced when she held the ice on the bump. She tried to stand up but fell back into the chair. "Do you see anything out of place?"

Annie looked around Christy's kitchen. "Not really." She opened the high cupboard where the computer was hidden. It was still there. She looked out the window at the raised bed. Nothing was disturbed. "Odd."

The dogs barked at the sound of tires in the driveway. "Now you bark," Christy said with irritation in her voice. "Why didn't you warn me when it was important?"

"That's a good question, Christy. Why didn't they bark?" Annie wondered out loud.

"Quick, Annie." Christy said. "Put Eddie's computer in my backpack. I want to keep it with me instead of leaving it here for someone else to get their hands on."

Annie stuffed the computer inside Christy's backpack seconds before Tyler's footsteps stomped toward the kitchen. He took one look at Christy and said, "I'm calling an ambulance."

"No!" Christy shouted. "I'm fine . . . well . . . I'll be fine. It's only a bump on my head. It's more important to figure out who did this."

Tyler pulled a chair close to Christy. "Any ideas?" he asked, his eyes full of concern.

"Someone connected to Eddie's murder and the scam. They must think I'm getting closer to putting it all together, or at least, I'm not going to give up and disappear on my own."

Tyler sat quietly, studying the kitchen. "Nothing was taken?"

Christy shook her head. "Not as far as I can tell."

"You could have been killed, you know. And yet, they only knocked you out."

"A warning?" Christy suggested.

Annie went to the sink to wash her hands. "Come and take a look at this. I don't want to touch it."

Tyler leaned around Annie's bent head. "Arsenic. I found a container exactly like this at the Catfish Cove Pub." He picked it up with a handkerchief and dropped it into a plastic evidence bag. "You'll have to stay someplace else while we go over your house with a fine tooth comb. With any luck, we'll find some fingerprints. Who's been here so we know who to eliminate?"

Christy looked up at the ceiling. "Me, Annie, Dusty, you, and maybe Jason. Did Jason come over with you the other day, Annie? I can't really remember."

Annie nodded.

"I can tell you whose fingerprints you shouldn't find—Samantha, Dennis, Kyle or Eddie, unless they were in here up to no good."

Tyler scribbled in his notebook. "Great. Do you have someplace you can stay?"

"Seriously? That's such an inconvenience," Christy's voice whined.

"You can stay at my apartment. Smokey will be glad for the company. Well, with your company, maybe not Bella and Blue, but he'll adjust."

Tyler nodded. "I like that idea. You won't be isolated with Jason and Annie right across the driveway. Pack up what you need to bring before the crew gets here to look for evidence. We'll test all your food to see if anything is contaminated."

Christy threw the ice in the sink. "The ice helped a lot. It's only sore if I touch it."

"So don't touch it!" Tyler scolded her.

She shot him a look as she walked by on her way to pack a few clothes.

Annie touched Tyler's arm. "What about the other arsenic bottle you found. At the pub?"

"It was in the dumpster behind the pub. Dennis swore he didn't know anything about it. No fingerprints, unfortunately. I suspect this bottle will be clean too, unless Christy surprised whoever was here and they made a careless mistake."

"Of course. But anyone walking by the dumpster could have thrown it in there. Finding this one in Christy's house has more significance, don't you think?"

Tyler nodded. "Yes. But let's hope my team finds more when they search the house."

Christy returned with her bulging backpack and she grabbed a cloth shopping bag for the dogs' food and bowls. "This should do it."

Annie helped Christy carry her stuff to her car. The dogs were excited to be outside and did some happy runs through the yard before they headed in opposite directions, sniffing.

"Come here Bella and Blue. Hop in the car." Christy held her car door open, waiting for the two dogs to finish up with their business and jump in. Blue was first in, taking the spot by the open window. Bella finally returned from behind the house shaking a piece of material like she wanted to kill it.

"What do you have?" Annie crouched down with her hand out. Bella held a chunk of denim in her mouth but she let Annie take it. "Any idea what this is from?" Annie held the material up so Christy could see it. "I hope she isn't chewing up your clothes."

"I made a tug for her with an old pair of jeans. Don't worry about it."

Annie tucked the fabric in her pocket. "Follow me," she said to Christy as she climbed into her car.

Annie got Christy and the two dogs settled in her apartment. Smokey disappeared out through his cat door as soon as the dogs bounded up the stairs.

"Will he be okay?" Christy asked, concern lacing her voice. "He has more right to be here than these two goofballs." She patted the dogs' heads.

"I'll see if I can find him and take him to Jason's house. He's not used to it over there, but he might decide it's quieter with the ones he knows rather than trying to get used to your two brutes." Annie started to walk out the door but turned around and said, "Come on over if you need company or food."

"I don't want to disturb you newly engaged lovebirds," Christy said with a laugh.

When Annie finally made it into Jason's house, her senses were rewarded with the crackling of burning wood in the fireplace, soft piano music playing, and a sweet cider smell.

Jason stood up from his piano. "I thought you skedaddled out of the state, never to be seen again." He wrapped his arms around Annie and pulled her close, whispering into her curls, "I missed you."

Her body relaxed and relished the comforting embrace. She felt lucky beyond words and safe in Jason's arms. "Skedaddled? Is that even a word?" she teased.

"Of course it is. A verb meaning to run away." He lowered his gaze to look into her eyes. "You have been known to skedaddle in the past if I'm not mistaken."

"No skedaddling; just a tad bit of, um, exploring. Oh, and by the way, Christy's staying in my apartment for a while," she added quickly in one breath before she walked to the kitchen. She poured herself a mug of the hot cider that made her mouth water with expectations of its sweet and tangy taste.

Jason remained leaning against the piano with his arms crossed and a half smile on his face. "I don't suppose Christy staying in my apartment has anything to do with Eddie's murder?"

Annie sipped the hot cider. "As a matter of fact, there could be a connection. Someone knocked her out cold and I found her on her kitchen floor."

Jason sat on his couch and patted the cushion next to him. "Start from the beginning and tell me everything. Don't leave one detail out," he told Annie and reinforced his words with his finger wagging in her direction.

Annie refilled her mug. "Do you want some cider too?"

"Please."

She settled comfortably in the crook of his shoulder and filled him in on all the information. It felt good to share the drama with Jason. With any luck, he might even think of a new angle that everyone else overlooked.

"Arsenic? Your poisoned punch theory was accurate?" Jason asked in awe of Annie's imagination being spot-on.

"I don't know how the poison got into Eddie's body, but Tyler found an arsenic bottle in the dumpster behind the pub and I found an arsenic bottle in Christy's sink. Tyler is at her house searching for more evidence. And that's the story in a nutshell, explaining why Christy and her dogs are now staying in my apartment."

"Eddie made some real nice friends at the bartender school," Jason said, his voice dripping with sarcasm.

"Uh huh. And, now, it appears that someone is after Christy." She snuggled closer to Jason. "Should we invite her over for something to eat?"

"Actually, I made other plans but she could tag along."

Annie stiffened. "We aren't leaving the house, are we?"

"Sort of. Leona invited us to the Catfish Cove Pub for a little engagement celebration."

Chapter 22

For a Sunday night, the Catfish Cove Pub was loud and busy. Jason held the door for Annie and she scanned the room. It wasn't hard to spot Leona. It never was. She let your eyes find the table with the most action.

Leona busily walked around the table filling mugs from a pitcher of beer. She straightened after each mug was filled, talking while her free arm waved wildly. Leona always managed to make every story sound exciting.

Annie waited until the pitcher was empty and sitting on the table before she poked Leona with two fingers on each side.

Leona twirled around "Of course it's you. You are the only one who manages to startle me." Leona hugged Annie before ushering her to an empty chair between

Camilla and Martha. "You don't mind if Jason sits next to *me*, do you?"

Annie rolled her eyes. "Why? So the two of you can do more scheming behind my back?"

Leona's laugh was her only response.

Annie draped her jacket over the back of the chair but headed to the ladies' room instead of making herself comfy at the table with her friends and family.

Quiet settled around her once the bathroom door closed. Not exactly how I expected to spend my evening, she thought, but maybe Jason and I can eat and run. While she was in the stall, she heard the bathroom door open and close.

"I thought you'd never finish up in there," Samantha joked when Annie finally emerged.

Annie washed her hands, watching Samantha's reflection in the mirror. Oddly,

Samantha remained leaning against the bathroom wall with her arms crossed. Annie could feel Samantha's eyes staring at her back, like hot pokers burning holes.

Icy fingers of fear worked their way up Annie's spine but she forced her voice to be strong. "Something on your mind, Samantha?" Annie dried her hands, her back still to Samantha.

Silence. Annie turned around.

"You and that detective have gotten kind of chummy." Samantha rubbed the earring dangling from her earlobe.

"And what about your friends? They don't strike me as a stellar bunch." Annie couldn't help digging for information about Dennis, Kyle, and Dusty.

Samantha looked away. "They're a bunch of fools. I had Eddie eating out of my hand. We were working on a plan but someone got greedy, and, well . . ."

"Someone what, Samantha? Someone killed Eddie? Is that what you left unsaid?"

A tear slid down her cheek. Her shoulders sagged. "Yes." All the bravado was gone from her voice. "Yes, someone killed Eddie."

Annie walked closer to Samantha. "Who? Do you know who killed Eddie?"

She shook her head. "I thought it was Christy." She spit out the name. "Eddie didn't trust her so I kept my eyes on what she was up to before her meeting with Eddie."

Annie's hand rested on Samantha's arm. "What do you mean?"

"I followed her on Halloween eve. She was on the Lake Trail, walking so fast I had trouble keeping up. I was watching when she met Eddie in that parking lot and stabbed him." Her tear-filled eyes stared at Annie. "He fell and she left." Samantha brushed the tears away. "When I rushed to his side, he was moaning and in bad shape, but he wasn't dead so I ran to get my car to take him home and patch him up."

"Are you sure he wasn't dead?" Annie asked.

Samantha nodded. "But when I got back, he was gone. I didn't know what to do so I left too. I went back to work and kept to the plan Eddie and I made. I was supposed to meet him in front of the cafe with Blue at eight o'clock to make the switch. Blue for the money."

"Did you see anyone else?"

She shook her head. "Not until I came back with Blue and all of you were looking for Eddie still." She covered her face with her hands. "I should have paid more attention, but I guess I panicked."

Annie held Samantha by both arms and shook her roughly. "*Look* at me. This is important. You said you went back to work but no one remembers seeing you at the pub the night Eddie was murdered."

"I had a costume on. We all rotated on and off behind the bar. It was so hectic, I don't think anyone paid attention to who was making the drinks."

"Who did you rotate with?

"Dennis, Dusty, and Kyle. We all took turns serving or mixing drinks. When it was my turn for a break, I got Blue and went to find Eddie."

"Everyone took breaks?"

"Yeah."

The bathroom door opened and three drunk girls stumbled in, laughing and gossiping about their dates. Annie and Samantha stood at the sinks waiting for privacy. The girls used the stalls, combed their hair, freshened their makeup, and didn't act like they were in any hurry to leave.

Samantha dried her hands and whispered to Annie, "I've got to get back to work, but there is something else I need to tell you." Then she turned and left, leaving Annie wondering what else Samantha knew.

Jason raised one eyebrow when Annie slid into her chair between Martha and Camilla. She avoided his look, at the moment, glad to be on the opposite side of the table.

Camilla whispered to Annie, "Dusty's working tonight. He keeps staring at me. Do you think I should talk to him?"

"Sure. What's the harm? But let him do all the talking and don't forgive him too quickly. Let him squirm and grovel for your forgiveness."

Camilla's lips turned up at the edges. "I don't know if I can do that but I'll give it my best shot. You know how words just flop out of my mouth when I'm around handsome men, and with the first sexy grin he offers, I'll be putty in his hands."

Annie squeezed Camilla's arm. "You can do it. Smile and say yes or no. He'll pick up the slack, and besides he's working, so there will be lots of interruptions."

Camilla put her shoulders back, which, of course, forced her best features forward, and she sashayed to the far end of the bar. Annie could see that Dusty had his eyes on the prize as he made his way to meet Camilla.

Jason stood up, working his way to Camilla's empty chair. "You were in the bathroom for an awfully long time; are you feeling okay?"

Annie leaned close, kissing his cheek before whispering in Jason's ear, "Samantha decided to share some information with me, but we were interrupted before she got to the interesting part."

Jason put his arm around her shoulder. "Be careful."

Samantha arrived with two large steaming pizzas fresh from the oven. Leona quickly moved empty pitchers and mugs to the edge of the table to make room.

Leona returned with a full pitcher and refilled all the empty mugs. "Listen up. One is the meat lover's pizza and the other is pesto, broccoli, tomato. Mozzarella sticks are on the way, too. Eat up before everything gets cold."

Jason slid a veggie slice onto his plate. "Which one do you want?" he asked Annie.

"They both look delicious. Probably one of each." She saw Jason's surprised look. "What? I'm hungry."

Samantha leaned between Jason and Annie, sliding a plate of mozzarella sticks onto the table. "Don't look now, but Dennis and Kyle are arguing. I think Dennis fired Kyle."

"Why?"

"Dennis accused Kyle of bringing attention to the pub because of the empty arsenic bottle."

Annie's eyes popped open wide after hearing that comment. "Aren't you living with Kyle?"

Samantha filled her tray with empty mugs. "Convenience. We aren't even very good friends." She headed back to the bar, stopping to check on customers at another table.

"What do you make of that revelation?" Annie asked Jason.

"You'd better find out if Tyler found any fingerprints before jumping to conclusions. Samantha could be trying to steer you in the wrong direction."

Martha bumped Annie on her shoulder. "What are you two whispering about over here?"

"Sorry Martha. Where's Harry tonight?"

She flicked her wrist. "He hates crowds. Says he gets claustrophobic. Between you and me? He's probably watching old westerns. He knows I hate them and he binge watches when I go out." She nodded her head toward the bar. "Camilla seems to be enjoying herself. She always gets the handsome ones."

Samantha returned with drinks for Annie and Jason. "Someone at your table ordered these in honor of your engagement."

Annie looked at Leona, who was grinning from ear to ear. She held her mug up and winked at Annie, mouthing, 'It's about time.'

A crash and a scream made everyone turn toward the bar. Dusty tore himself away from Camilla's beguiling smile and rushed to separate Kyle and Dennis before more fists were thrown between the two.

Kyle's angry voice carried through the now mostly quiet pub. "You've got it all wrong,

Dennis, and I'll prove it. It was Eddie and Samantha planning to double-cross *you*."

Annie stood up, searching for Samantha. She had been right next to Annie when the commotion began. Annie wanted answers from Samantha about what Kyle meant. Her head twisted around, back and forth, but Samantha was nowhere to be found in the pub.

Jason held Annie's arm. "I know what you're thinking, but you aren't leaving to look for Samantha. She's been feeding you information and now she's disappeared. Something doesn't add up with her stories. It's time to let Tyler handle everything."

"Samantha could think she's in danger— maybe even the next victim. What did Kyle mean about proving Dennis had it all wrong? Had *what* wrong?"

Jason held Annie tighter. "I don't know, but this is escalating to a dangerous level."

Annie felt a hand on her shoulder. She turned away from Jason to see Christy at her side. "I didn't think you were coming tonight."

Christy twisted her head back and forth, searching the pub. "It wasn't my plan but Tyler texted me to meet him here. What's going on?"

Chapter 23

"Chaos," Annie said. "Dennis fired Kyle and they got into a fight. Dusty broke it up and now Samantha has disappeared. Did Tyler discover something?"

"Your guess is as good as mine, but here he comes to explain."

The customers in the pub were all back to laughing and drinking as if nothing had happened moments earlier. Dennis's offer to everyone for a complimentary beer helped to ease the transition. For almost everyone.

Christy pulled Tyler to a corner table. Annie and Jason slid in too.

"Okay, what's going on?" Christy asked. "Why did you tell me to meet you here?"

"I found a small notebook tucked under the mattress in Eddie's apartment. I don't know how we missed it the first time.

Anyway, it's filled with lists of phone numbers, and your number is on the list."

Annie noticed Christy flinch and tense her jaw muscles. She shrugged. "So what? Eddie knew my number. I never changed it when I left him."

"We think the other numbers are people who were scammed. There are dollar amounts after the phone numbers. Where's the money?"

Christy stood up but kept her hands flat on the table as she leaned mere inches from Tyler's face. "The. Money. Is. Safe. When this spectacle is over, you'll get the money." Her head nodded slightly toward the bar. "They have to think I still have it or we won't be able to flush them out."

Tyler and Christy stared at each other, neither one wanting to be the first to back down. Christy won.

"I don't like it, but short of arresting you, I'll go along with your plan. For now." He checked the time on his watch. "I'll give you the rest of today to come up with something solid. That's only a few hours."

Christy scowled and left.

Annie touched Tyler's hand, hoping to relieve some of the tension. "Does she know what she's doing?"

Tyler's shoulders sagged. "I hope so."

"There's more bad news. Samantha has disappeared." Annie filled Tyler in on the drama behind the bar before he arrived.

He ran his fingers through his already disheveled hair. "Don't they live together, Kyle and Samantha?"

"They do, but Samantha told me they aren't even friends. It's just for convenience."

Tyler's hand traveled from his hair to his chin. "I need a shave."

Annie took notice of the dark circles under his eyes. "Not getting much sleep?"

"I've barely even been home with all that's happening." He stood up. "With any luck, maybe I can round up Kyle and Samantha at their apartment. Any idea where else they would go?"

Annie shook her head. "Do you think they could be running together?"

"It wouldn't surprise me. We did find prints on the arsenic bottle at Christy's house. Kyle's. I'll be back to question Dennis and Dusty after I find those other two."

Jason and Annie joined the rest of their group at the big table. They were barely missed with all the talking and eating. Camilla returned to the table with a big smile on her face.

"I think things are back on track with Dusty," she whispered to Annie.

"Oh? How so?"

"He invited me for dinner tomorrow night. What do you think?"

"Sounds nice." Annie answered half-heartedly, her mind on other problems.

The pub was beginning to thin out. Dusty busied himself wiping tables while Dennis stayed behind the bar. Annie didn't have the heart to tell Camilla that with Kyle and Samantha missing, there was a good chance Dusty would be working instead of taking her to dinner.

Jason bumped Annie with his elbow. "Hey, ready to go?"

"Is there any pizza left?"

Jason opened the box. One cold piece sat inside. "Are you still hungry?"

Annie nodded.

He took her hand. "Come on, there's still plenty of food in my refrigerator. You can have some dessert and we'll take Roxy for a walk.

It took longer to leave with all the goodbyes and hugs, but finally they made it outside into the crisp night air.

"I wonder where Christy is," Annie said more to herself than to Jason.

He put his arm around her. "She's probably curled up on the couch in your apartment with her two dogs. Did you ever find Smokey?"

"No. That will be my first priority when we get back."

"Okay. I'll make a fire while you find Smokey and bring him over."

Annie dashed ahead of Jason. "Last one to the car has to do the dishes." With her head start, she easily beat Jason to the car, leaning on it while laughing and trying to catch her breath. "*Loser*," she taunted.

"I let you win this time," he said and wrapped her in his arms. "I've already won the best prize."

"Nice try, Mr. Hunter, but I won fair and square."

Jason unlocked the car doors and opened the passenger side for Annie, whispering in her ear, "You can believe whatever makes you happy."

Jason pulled into his driveway next to Christy's car.

Nodding toward Christy's car, Annie said, "I wasn't sure she would be here. She seemed pretty mad after her conversation with Tyler. I think I'll look for Smokey and leave Christy alone to sort out her problems."

"Good idea," Jason answered as he headed to his door and Annie walked toward the lake.

Roxy bounded out when Jason opened the door, catching up with Annie. "Come on Roxy, help me find Smokey." She lit the path with her flashlight, swinging it from side to side, hoping to see Smokey.

Annie called to her kitty, not convinced Smokey even wanted to be found. Not far from her apartment, Annie heard a faint mewing. She pushed branches aside, inching her way along the Lake Trail searching under all the bushes. The mewing got louder and the bushes got denser.

"Smokey, here kitty, kitty," Annie called. She could hear Smokey but couldn't see him in the thick, dark brush. She got down on her hands and knees and shined her light into the tangled mess where she thought Smokey was hiding. She crawled in as far as possible.

Annie's bottom was sticking out into the path and her hair got tangled in the sharp branches as she reached toward Smokey. His eyes reflected in the flashlight but he wouldn't budge.

"Are you all right Annie?"

This is awkward, she thought to herself. "Um, sort of. Is that you Dusty?"

"It is. What are you doing?"

"I'm trying to rescue my kitty but I can't reach him." Her fingers touched Smokey's fur but she couldn't get a grip on him to pull him out.

"Let me try. My arms are longer."

The branches moved and poked into Annie as Dusty crawled in next to her. "I see him." Dusty reached toward Smokey and was rewarded with sharp claws in his hand. "Ouch! But I have him. I'll pull him to you and you can get him out the rest of the way before I lose too much blood."

Smokey yowled in protest. Dusty managed to move him enough so Annie could wrap her hands around his body and wiggle back out from under the bush.

"Thank you so much, Dusty. I'm not sure I could have gotten him without your help."

"No problem." He brushed twigs and leaves off his jacket and wiped his bloody hand on his jeans.

"Is your hand okay?"

He inspected it. "It'll be fine. Just a couple of puncture holes. Why was he hiding in there anyway?"

Annie cradled Smokey and started to walk back toward Jason's house. "Christy's staying in my apartment for a day or two and Smokey, here, wasn't too crazy about having her dogs as roommates."

Dusty laughed. "I don't blame him. Do you know where Christy is? I need to talk to her."

Annie looked in the driveway. "That's strange. Her car was here when I got back, maybe a half hour ago. I didn't talk to her so I don't know where she went. Did you discover something new?"

"I think so. I'll check at her house. Do you want to come with me?"

"Sure. Wait a minute while I put Smokey and Roxy inside."

Annie called Roxy and carried Smokey into Jason's house. Smokey wandered around sniffing, investigating the new surroundings before he jumped into the recliner and curled up. Annie heard the shower running so she scribbled a note for Jason and tucked it under the bottle of wine sitting on the counter. *Be right back. Checking up on Christy.* There, now he can't accuse me of skedaddling on him, she thought proudly.

Dusty had the car on and the heater blasting when Annie slid into the passenger seat. "What's going on?"

"I need Christy's help to find Samantha and Kyle."

"Tyler didn't find them?"

Dusty backed the car from the driveway. "Apparently, they bolted."

Annie willed the car to go faster but Dusty poked along at the speed limit. Were Kyle and Samantha at Christy's house?

Chapter 24

Christy's street was quiet, her car in the driveway as Dusty slowly drove by. Slivers of light showed at the edges of her curtains. Dusty turned off his car and coasted to a stop just out of sight of Christy's house. "We can walk in the shadows, so in case anyone is watching, they won't see us."

Annie nodded. She wrapped her fingers around the flashlight in her pocket. Just in case. She didn't know what to expect and she was glad to have Dusty in front of her as they silently tiptoed closer to Christy's house.

Since she couldn't see much, her ears worked overtime. A rustling in the bushes made them both pause and hold their breath. A skunk wandered in front of them, but hurried on its way without coating them in its perfume.

Annie kept one hand on Dusty's back for reassurance. A car crept along the street. Annie thought it looked like Samantha driving.

Dusty whispered, "I think that's Kyle's car. We'd better hurry inside."

Annie forced herself to breathe and wondered why on earth she was even here instead of sitting with Jason in front of his fire. But Christy was her friend and might need help. Wasn't that what friends were for?

They reached Christy's back door. Through the window, Annie could see Christy at her kitchen counter, absorbed in front of Eddie's computer. Dusty tapped softly on the glass until Christy heard the noise. Her eyes were wide with worry until she saw who it was and she quickly let them in.

"What are you two doing here? I thought I'd be able to work out this puzzle alone." She stood with her hands on her hips, not exactly the welcome Annie was expecting.

"I was worried," Dusty explained. "Kyle and Samantha could be out there cooking up something."

"What about Dennis?"

"He's still at the pub, cleaning and closing up." Dusty looked over Christy's shoulder at the computer. "Find anything?"

"Yeah. I'm starting to think Eddie was the mastermind of the scam which would explain why he held onto the money. Listen to this." Christy opened a new recipe labeled *Grandma's Stew*. " 'Sam is leading the way. Conned a new one today out of ten thousand. At this rate, we can move on soon.' Every recipe in this folder is actually a new amount of money they conned someone out of." She looked up at Dusty and Annie, shaking her head. "This makes my blood boil."

Suddenly, the back door was pushed open.

Three pair of eyes turned to see Samantha holding a gun on them.

"Samantha?" Annie asked in total shock.

Dusty inched away, leaving Christy and Annie between Samantha and himself.

"Nice work, Dusty. I wanted both of them together. Get the money and finish them off," Samantha sneered.

"Dusty?" Christy asked in disbelief. "You're working with *her*?"

He slid Christy's gun off the table. "Sorry. Tell us where the money is and no one will get hurt."

Samantha waved her gun between Christy and Annie. "That's not how we planned it, Dusty. They know too much."

"No! You killed Eddie, that's enough. No more killing."

Annie felt her knees go weak. Her brain could not process this turn of events. She thought Samantha was the one in trouble. What a fool she was to believe her stories. Jason was right about Samantha manipulating her with all her tears and suspicions about the others.

"How'd you do it Samantha?" Christy asked in a low, almost hypnotizing voice. "How'd you kill Eddie? Did he *plead* with you? Promise you the *world*?"

"That fool. He was still in love with you. It was so easy, especially when you helped him along by stabbing him. At the rate the arsenic was working, he would have lasted a few more days. And that stupid dog of yours. I couldn't get rid of him fast enough."

"And the arsenic bottle in my house?" Annie knew what Christy was doing. Keep Samantha talking, stroke her ego, and make her feel smarter than she was.

"Ha, I pressed Kyle's finger on the bottle when he was passed out drunk one night. Brilliant, right?"

Christy nodded.

Annie watched Dusty from the corner of her eye. He pulled rope from his jacket pocket.

"Enough talking. Come over here you two." Dusty directed Annie and Christy to sit in two kitchen chairs with their hands around the backs of the chairs.

Annie felt the rope tighten, almost cutting off her circulation, then it slacked a bit. What was he doing?

Samantha closed Eddie's laptop and slid it into her backpack. "You won't be needing this anymore. Now, the money."

"Shoot me," Christy said. "You'll never find it."

Annie almost wet her pants. "I don't want to die. Tell her where you buried it."

Samantha laughed. "Buried it, huh? No problem. We can start digging up your yard."

"There's no time for that, Samantha. We have to get out of here," Dusty said. "Where is it Christy? You don't want to watch Samantha shoot Annie first, do you?"

Christy lashed out at Dusty with her foot but missed. "Samantha leaves and I'll tell you. I don't trust her. She'll get the money and shoot us anyway."

"I might too," Dusty threatened.

"I'll take my chances." They stared with angry eyes at each other.

"She stays but I'll hold the gun." Dusty took the gun from Samantha and aimed it at Annie. "Where is it, Christy?"

"I wish you would learn to listen better, Annie. I told you to stay out of this." She twisted her shoulders, making the chair tip precariously on one leg, but it landed upright.

"Are you done with your temper tantrum?" Dusty asked.

"It's in the closet." Her head nodded toward the door at right angles to the stove. "Buried under all the dog food."

Annie's mouth fell open. "You said it was buried in your raised bed."

"No. *You* said it was buried there, I never agreed with your assumption."

Samantha dashed to the closet and yanked the door open. A large plastic tub sat under the bottom shelf. She slid the tub from the closet and threw the lid off, tipping the base so dog food spilled all over Christy's gleaming kitchen floor.

"Where are the dogs when I need them?" she said. "They'd have a field day with this mess."

Samantha pulled out a black garbage bag and looked inside. She whistled when she reached inside, holding up a stack of money. "Nice, all hundreds it looks like. Eddie wasn't kidding when he told me we'd be rich." She laughed.

"*You?* He was planning to split it with *you?*" Dusty said with disgust.

"Uh huh, and I wasn't thrilled with that part of the plan. Too bad he had that unfortunate accident and won't be around to enjoy this with me." She cackled. "It would have been better if Christy had finished him off, but it wasn't much trouble to push him onto that cement wall and make sure he was finally dead." She stood up and heaved the bag filled with money over her shoulder. "Let's go. Make sure those two won't wiggle loose any time soon. I have a car hidden for the get-a-way."

Dusty held out his free hand for the bag of money. "I can carry that."

"Right! I don't *think* so. *You've* got the gun. *I've* got the cash." Samantha headed for the door without a glance back. She had what she came for and Dusty better keep up if he wanted his share.

Silence filled Christy's kitchen like a tomb.

"What do we do now?" Annie asked.

"They won't get far. The computer has a tracking device and Dusty didn't know about that."

A gunshot tore through the silence. Annie's heart felt like it burst apart. "Did he shoot her?"

Chapter 25

"I don't think so," Christy said while she fiddled with the rope tying her hands together, shaking them free. "I'll need to teach Dusty how to tie better knots."

"What? We won't see him again," Annie said, her voice filled with disgust.

"Don't count on it."

Christy grabbed her phone. "Tyler? They're on their way."

Annie pulled against the rope tying her hands and yelled at Christy. "Christy Crank! Untie me right now and tell me what craziness is going on."

"Not until you promise to stay calm." Christy stood in front of Annie with her hands on her hips.

"Calm? You could have gotten us killed. Well, at the moment I don't think I could care less if Samantha shot you, but I'm not ready to die."

Christy laughed. "Thanks a lot. And I thought we were friends." She untied Annie's hands. "You better call Jason and tell him you're okay. I had to let him in on the plan to make sure he didn't follow you over here and mess everything up."

"What plan?" Christy had her attention as she rubbed some feeling back into her hands.

Dusty walked inside, laughing. A faint whiff of skunk followed him.

Annie froze.

"You should have seen the look on Samantha's face when the skunk scooted out from under her car. I pretended to try to shoot it, but," he looked at his gun, "it doesn't help when it's loaded with blanks. She got a direct squirt of skunk, threw the money in the car and hightailed it down the street without even checking if I was following her."

Christy bent over, she was laughing so hard. "Poor Tyler. He'll blame me for having to transport a skunky prisoner." She looked at Annie. "The skunk wasn't part of the plan, but I like the timing."

Annie grabbed Christy's arm. "Tell. Me. What's. Going. On. *Now*," she demanded through gritted teeth.

The grin on Dusty's face evaporated. "She doesn't know?"

"Nope. I haven't had a chance to fill her in yet." She looked at Annie. "Call Jason first, then we'll explain everything."

Annie took a deep breath. A very deep breath. She filled her lungs and slowly let the air back out. She repeated the process and started to feel calmer. At least, calm enough to call Jason. He said he'd be right over.

Christy brought three beers to the table, handing one to Annie and one to Dusty. "I think we deserve this while we wait for Jason."

"How did Dusty get blanks into Samantha's gun?"

Christy flicked her wrist. "It was his gun."

"And you knew?"

"Of course." Christy took a long swallow of the beer. "I was parched. This tastes great."

"Start at the beginning, please." Annie finally sipped her beer and felt her body start to relax.

Dusty and Christy both pulled out chairs and joined Annie at the table.

"I figured out that Eddie was the mastermind and, with Dusty working behind the scenes, we decided Samantha was the easiest participant to manipulate into being his partner to steal the money from me. Of course, Samantha loved the idea of splitting all the money between just the two of them."

"So, all that crap Samantha told me—"

Christy interrupted, "Yeah, all crap. She played you like a cheap violin."

The back door opened and three hyper dogs rushed inside, followed by Jason. "Thought I'd bring your dogs back." Roxy jumped all over Annie while Blue and Bella slobbered on Christy.

Jason helped himself to a beer from Christy's fridge. "Everything went as planned?"

Christy nodded. "Like a well-oiled machine. Thanks for helping."

Annie glared. "I can't believe you were all in on this and let me think I was about to have my head blown off."

Christy patted Annie's arm. "You played the most important role. Samantha had to believe she had you wrapped around her finger with all her sob stories. We couldn't risk having her suspect you didn't believe her."

"Nice try to make me feel better about being completely blindsided tonight, but it's not working."

Christy's phone rang. "Okay," she said and hung up. "Tyler wants us all to come down to the station."

Jason stood behind Annie with his hands protectively on her shoulders. "You can come with me. A little distance from Christy will do you good."

Christy chuckled. "I thought it was a lot of fun."

Annie followed Jason to his car and opened the back for Roxy to jump in.

"It smells like skunk out here," Jason said as he sniffed the air.

Annie finally started to laugh. The combination of stress, adrenaline and the absurdity of Dusty trying to shoot a skunk knowing the gun was loaded with blanks made her break down into hysterical laughing and crying.

"It's only a skunk," Jason said, shaking his head in confusion.

Annie leaned on the car. "Yeah, it's only a skunk. The skunk and I weren't in on the plan." She looked at Jason. "I made it out alive and I'm glad the skunk got away to spray someone else another night."

Everyone at the police station had their hands covering their noses. Annie started to laugh again, but this time, it was only a giggle that she didn't let get out of control.

Tyler informed Annie that Samantha, Kyle, and Dennis were all in his custody, and with the money recovered and the notebook he found in Eddie's apartment, all the money would be returned to the victims. "It was complicated, but everything worked out in the end."

"And the skunk got away," she added.

***

After a hot shower, Annie curled up under the down comforter and fell asleep two seconds after her head hit the pillow. No dreams, just pure, restful sleep.

The smell of coffee hit her nose even before her eyes opened. Sun filtered through the curtains and she stretched under the covers, thinking about the skunk that got away. She smiled.

Jason walked in carrying a tray with coffee, one yellow sunflower, and a pumpkin scone.

"Feeling guilty?" Annie asked, her lips curled up at the edges. She scooched up higher with pillows behind her back.

"A little. Especially after I lectured you to stop keeping secrets from me." Jason sat on the bed and rested the tray across her legs.

She broke off a piece of the scone. "Mmmm. I could get used to this treatment." She sipped her coffee. "Perfect." After setting the cup down, she asked, "How did they talk you into being part of the scheme?"

"It wasn't easy. Tyler and Dusty ganged up on me. Dusty was positive that Samantha was about to make her move, and if he wasn't part of the plan, the gun would have had real bullets." Jason stared into Annie's eyes. "I know Tyler wouldn't let anything bad happen to you. I thanked him for that."

Jason stood up. "You might want to think about getting dressed soon. Company's on the way over."

Annie sat up, sloshing the coffee over the edge of the cup. "You're kidding, right?"

"Not kidding." Jason's eyes crinkled at the corners. "Do you want to finish your coffee or should I bring it back downstairs?"

Annie sighed. "I was so looking forward to a quiet and peaceful morning." She handed the tray to Jason. "I'll be down soon."

Annie found her comfy, worn-in blue jeans and a soft flannel shirt. She looked in the mirror and gave her hair a quick comb. Good enough for me, she thought, so good enough for whoever is coming over this early.

The sound of chattering voices grew louder with each step she took down the stairs. Of course, Leona was the first one to spot her.

"Don't you have any decent clothes to wear over here?" she asked as her eyes traveled over Annie's casual outfit.

Annie ignored the comment. "What brings you over so bright and early? Is the café out of business?"

"Of course not, I like opening a little later during the week at this time of year."

Jason approached Annie and put his arm around her waist. "Leona brought over a feast. Come and have a look."

Platters of scrambled eggs, hash browns, corn bread, and fruit salad filled Jason's dining room table. "There's enough for an army." She looked around the room at all the people staring at her.

"Help yourselves before the food gets cold!" She picked up a plate for herself and loaded it with some of everything.

Conversations started up again and Annie was happy to blend into the background with Jason by her side while she enjoyed Leona's delicious cooking.

"Hope you don't mind that I'm here too?"

Annie blinked. Then blinked again. Dusty stood in front of her, smiling his incredibly engaging smile. "Surprised, I guess. Your project here in town is done so I assumed you'd be leaving."

Dusty glanced toward Camilla then back to Annie. "I kind of like the scenery here and I've got a new project to work on."

"Oh?"

"I heard there will be a pub in town looking for a new owner."

Annie smiled. "And a certain blonde doesn't have anything to do with your decision?"

Dusty actually blushed. "Ah, yes, a little, and she said I need your approval."

Annie's hand flew to her mouth to catch the food that was about to fly out when she burst out laughing. She kept one eye on Camilla. "She said that, did she?"

Camilla rushed over to Annie's side. "What do you think?" Her eyes were wide with anticipation.

"He didn't shoot the skunk so that makes him okay in my book."

"That reminds me," Jason turned around and handed a gift bag to Annie, "Christy is working but she asked me to give this to you."

Annie's eyes narrowed to slits. "Is it safe to stick my hand inside?"

Jason nodded, trying to control the quiver of his lips.

Annie stuck her hand in the bag. "It's soft." She looked at the three faces watching her as she pulled out a stuffed animal and laughed out loud. "A skunk," she said between her fits of laughter. "Perfect."

With Halloween approaching, my daughter called me and put 5 year old Mark on the phone. He asked if I could make him a Halloween costume. That sounded like a fun project so I asked what he had in mind.

"Well, you know how I love superheroes?" Mark asked.

"Yes, I do, and Danny loves them too," I answered, wondering what I was getting myself into.

"Can you make us capes?" His voice coming through the phone was full of hope.

"Okay. That doesn't sound too hard. How about Superman and Spiderman?" I knew they had underwear with those superheroes.

He yelled a loud yes so we made a date and I bought the supplies I would need.

When I arrived at their house with two capes in hand, Danny asked, "What about baby Emma? Can she be a superhero too?"

I smiled at his thoughtfulness. "Of course. I already planned something for her." I reached into my bag and pulled out a long sleeve purple onesie with a black bat stenciled on the front. "How about if Emma is Batgirl?"

"Yeah, yeah, yeah. She'll like that." Mark held the onesie up so Emma could see it and she smiled. Of course, she always smiles when she sees someone's face, but Mark was positive it meant she liked the costume.

With Emma happy, I fastened the capes to Mark and Danny. They dashed around their house in true superhero fashion while I got set up to make a Halloween treat for them. By the time I was ready, they were curious what I was doing so I pulled two chairs up to the counter so they could help me make:

Boysenberry Punch

I measured two cups of frozen boysenberries, 1 cup for each grandson to dump into the blender. I added 2 cups of water and let Mark turn the blender on. They loved watching the mixture turn into a deep maroon color.

Danny stared at the swirling liquid before asking, "Are you making Poisonberry Punch, Mimi?"

I laughed out loud. "No, it's *boys*enberry, but we can change the name if you want to."

They both looked at me with big grins and said, "Yes!"

"Okay. Next," I told them, "I have to dump in a 12 ounce can of frozen lemonade." It was Danny's turn to turn the blender on and we watched as everything mixed together.

I poured this into a big glass pitcher, adding a 1 liter bottle of plain seltzer.

With our punch ready, I carried 5 tall glasses to the table for Mark, Danny, their mom, dad and myself. I also brought a big plate of sugar cookies to go with the punch. Halloween shapes and colors of course!

When everyone was sitting, I poured the punch into glasses filled with ice and added extra boysenberries on top for a garnish.

The boys each chose a pumpkin cookie frosted with orange icing and chocolate chips forming a face.

Danny sipped his drink, declaring, "It's delicious Poisonberry Punch, Mimi!"

I hope you enjoy Halloween as much as we do, and be sure to try some Poisonberry Punch too!

Cheers

~Lyndsey

ABOUT THE AUTHOR

Lyndsey Cole lives in New England in a small rural town with her husband, dogs, cats and chickens. She has plenty of space to grow lots of beautiful perennials. Sitting in the garden with the scent of lilac, peonies, lily of the valley or whatever is in bloom, stimulates her imagination about mysteries and romance.

ONE LAST THING . . .

If you enjoyed this installment of The Black Cat Café Cozy Mystery Series, be sure to join my FREE COZY MYSTERY BOOK CLUB! Be in the know for new releases, promotions, sales, and the possibility to receive advanced reader copies. Join the club here—http://LyndseyColeBooks.com

OTHER BOOKS BY LYNDSEY COLE

The Black Cat Café Series

BlueBuried Muffins

Annie Fisher is scared. She's scared of the mess her boyfriend, Max Parker, is in the middle of and she has to get out of his house. She puts a whole state between them and drives like a madwoman from Cooper, NY to her hometown of Catfish Cove, NH where she hopes she'll be safe.

She decides to start a new life, a life she ran away from two years ago but is finding herself missing as soon as she gets home. Annie immediately has a place to live, a job at her Aunt Leona's new café—Black Cat Café—and plenty of boyfriend prospects. Unfortunately, she also has plenty of bad things follow her.

Like Max Parker. Only the next time she sees him he's dead. Suddenly everyone she runs into turns into a potential suspect. There are ghosts from her past and new neighbors that make her hair stand on end.

And right in the middle of everything is Annie with Max's last warning to her—Don't trust anyone. Will those words prove to keep her safe or put too much distance between Annie and those trying to help her?

StrawBuried in Chocolate

Annie Fisher wakes up on Friday the thirteenth, but she reminds herself she's not superstitious. The Black Cat Café is loaded up with special Valentine's Day goodies, the most popular being Annie's chocolate covered strawberries. She is so looking forward to a romantic weekend with current flame, landlord and neighbor, Jason Hunter.

But when her Aunt Leona finds a body in Jason's house, all plans for that romantic weekend are scrapped. All Annie, Leona, Mia and Jason can think about is who killed Lacy McGuire and why.

With more and more clues pointing toward Leona as the killer, they need to work fast to figure out who the real killer is before Leona ends up in jail for good. To complicate matters for Annie, information surfaces about her birth parents, a mystery she's been working on for the past few years. She thinks she wants to find the answers, but will it destroy her world?

Now, Annie must struggle to save her aunt, but as she questions neighbors and relatives, will she put herself in danger with the real killer? Will she save her aunt but get herself killed in the process?

BlackBuried Pie

The Fourth of July weekend promises lots of excitement for the cozy town of Catfish Cove. A dog parade, bonfire, barbecue and fireworks are sure to bring in the crowds and give a boost to all businesses, including the Black Cat Café.

To prepare for the onslaught of customers, Annie Fisher has to keep their supply up of blackberries from Hayworth Fruit Farms for everyone's favorite, blackberry pie. But when she finds the berry farmer unconscious in his field, her mind immediately goes to the worst possible scenario. To make matters worse, the farmer's neighbor turns up dead and anonymous messages drag Annie into the mystery when all she wants to do is spend time with her handsome boyfriend.

With clues pointing in every direction, Annie needs to figure out who's lying and who she can trust before she ends up as the next victim in the killer's web of deceit.

Very Buried Cheesecake

This should be an exciting time for Annie with the opening of her new art gallery, but she's stressed and distracted preparing for her first photography opening. With her friend Martha and her new employee, Camilla, working to get the gallery set up, everything seems to be on track.

But when Annie stumbles on a body floating at the edge of Heron Lake, her worst fears are realized. Memories of her previous photography exhibit and the ensuing murder investigation come back to haunt her.

To make matters worse, the new detective in town points her finger at Annie right from their first meeting at the crime scene. Is this an ominous sign of what's in store for Annie? With mysterious money disappearing and stolen jewelry showing up from thin air, a pre wedding dinner cruise and Martha's on again/off again wedding, all is not what it seems.

Now Annie struggles to avoid being sucked into the mayhem. Will she be able to put her fears aside and figure out how to stay ahead of the killer?

RaspBuried Torte

When renovations on an old house in Catfish Cove take a turn for the worse, Annie finds herself at odds with the new detective in town. Again. Not only did Annie find the body, but Detective Christy Crank seems to have a chip on her shoulder that she takes out on Annie.

Rumors of hidden fortunes in the walls of the old house bring out treasure hunters in droves. Could one of them have killed to secure their own fortune? And if so, who was it?

As Annie digs deeper to clear the name of her friend, and Cranky's top suspect, Danny Davis, she uncovers lies about alibis that only add more suspects to her list. Dreams of wealth make plenty of people look guilty, but who is the real murderer?

Annie knows she has to figure it out with the help of her friends before Danny takes the fall for something he didn't do. Will she make it in time before the killer comes back to cover their tracks?

The Lily Bloom Series

Begonias Mean Beware

Misty Valley has a new flower shop in town, and as soon as Lily Bloom hangs the open sign, she lands the biggest wedding in town. Plus, the handsome new guy moves in right next door to Lily. She's well on her way to a successful and exciting season.

But when the groom is found dead in her kitchen just days before he's supposed to be walking down the aisle, Lily has to arrange the trail of flowers to try to solve the mystery. With the help of her scooter-riding, pot-smoking mother, Iris, her sister, Daisy, and her dog, Rosie, Lily races from one disaster to another, all the while keeping herself out of the killer's sight.

Will she solve the cascade of events in time or get caught by the criminals running illegal gambling and selling drugs in Misty Valley? Will romance blossom between Lily and her new neighbor?

Queen of Poison

Business at Lily's Beautiful Blooms Flower Shop is growing like weeds after a rainstorm. She's been asked to do the main flower arrangement for the Arts in Bloom opening at the Misty Valley Museum. Everything seems to be coming up rosy and she's even falling head over heels for the man of her dreams, Ryan Steele, her neighbor and the police chief of Misty Valley.

Until she sees a sleek red convertible drive into his driveway. And an even sleeker red head climbs out of the car. She thought that was all she had to deal with until the founder of the museum drops dead in her arms and another body has all fingers pointing toward Lily.

With help from her mom, Iris, her sister, Daisy and their friends Marigold and Tamara, Lily tries to arrange the clues to point to the real killer. Can she sort it out in time before a third body—maybe hers—ends up in the morgue? Can she get her romance growing again with the handsome police chief of Misty Valley? Or will she be left to sort through the clues alone?

Roses are Dead

Business is popping for Lily as wedding season is in full swing. The brides are all over the place from easy-to-please to last-minute-panics. But one in particular stands out—a leggy brunette who is looking for plenty of red roses for her wedding to Police Chief Ryan Steele.

Lily is beside herself with betrayal that Ryan would lead her on like that, all the while engaged to this beauty. It's almost too much to take until the bride is found dead, surrounded by none other than the very roses she'd been admiring.

Lily shoots to the top of the suspect list, a place she's been all too often lately. And as she starts to uncover more about the woman's past, she's thrown into another game of cat and mouse. Only she's not sure if she's the cat or the mouse. Will she be able to follow the clues to the real killer in time? Or is everyone connected to Ryan Steele in danger and Lily could be next?

Drowning in Dahlias

The business is heating up at Beautiful
Blooms and Lily's flower arrangements can
be found all over Misty Valley at any type of
event. And to add to the chaos, she's lost
the full time help of her sister, Daisy, who
has started a specialty cake making
business on the side. Together, they make
the perfect team, especially when wealthy
estate owner, Walter Nash, enlists both of
them to cater and decorate for the 55th
birthday party for his wife.

But when they show up with their
deliveries and find the love of his life,
Harriet Nash, dead on the floor, the
dynamic duo is suddenly threatened. With
a house full of family and friends to
celebrate her birthday, there are too many
suspects to keep straight.

Lily's biggest challenge now is to find the
killer before the killer finds her. But
without a murder weapon at the crime
scene, the questions continue to pile up
without any answers. Who would have

wanted Harriet dead the most? She had plenty of money, but would someone have been so greedy? As Lily and Daisy get closer to solving the murder, things take a turn for the worse with a threat on Lily's life.

Hidden by the Hydrangeas

Lily Bloom can't seem to keep her thoughts away from marriage. Maybe it's just because her mom tied the knot with her childhood sweetheart Walter Nash, but it's gotten Lily thinking about her own relationship with Ryan Steele and if it's going anywhere.

But those thoughts are quickly replaced with who is carrying a dead body, and who that dead body might be. The only thing Lily knows is that she's been spotted by the killer so she has to hope this mystery is solved before she's the next one in a body bag.

When Walter's best friend turns up as the likeliest suspect, Lily's mom is beside herself with worry and convinces Lily that she's the best person to solve this case. But suspects keep piling up with not quite enough evidence to prove anything. Will Lily be able to put all the pieces together before the killer sniffs out her trail?

Christmas Tree Catastrophe

Lily Bloom couldn't be more excited for Christmas Eve when she will say "I do" to the man she loves. She just has the library opening to get through and then all the town's focus will be on her.

But things start going wrong almost from the very first moment she's getting setup for the library's event. Not only is there plenty of disagreement among those helping, but one of the co-chairs who is in charge of the whole event winds up dead the day before the ceremony.

With everyone who was helping setup under a microscope, Lily is in a race against time to be able to get married. When one of her best friends winds up in jail for the murder Lily knows she didn't commit, the pressure's on to find the real murderer.

Will Lily be able to prove her friend's innocence? Or will she find herself in even more trouble and face a wedding in a jail cell or the hospital? Or worse—will there be no wedding at all because the bride is the new target?

Made in the USA
Lexington, KY
29 September 2015